Chaos in the Cauldron

A Witch Lit Romance

First published by Treehouse Magic 2019

Copyright © 2019 by Sheena Cundy

All rights reserved. No part of this publication may be reproduced, stored or transmitted in any form or by any means, electronic, mechanical, photocopying, recording, scanning, or otherwise without written permission from the publisher. It is illegal to copy this book, post it to a website, or distribute it by any other means without permission.

This novel is entirely a work of fiction. The names, characters and incidents portrayed in it are the work of the author's imagination. Any resemblance to actual persons, living or dead, events or localities is entirely coincidental.

Sheena Cundy asserts the moral right to be identified as the author of this work.

Sheena Cundy has no responsibility for the persistence or accuracy of URLs for external or third-party Internet Websites referred to in this publication and does not guarantee that any content on such Websites is, or will remain, accurate or appropriate.

Designations used by companies to distinguish their products are often claimed as trademarks. All brand names and product names used in this book and on its cover are trade names, service marks, trademarks and registered trademarks of their respective owners. The publishers and the book are not associated with any product or vendor mentioned in this book. None of the companies referenced within the book have endorsed the book.

First edition

This book was professionally typeset on Reedsy.
Find out more at reedsy.com

*For the Goddesses.
You know who you are.*

Chaos is a friend of mine.

BOB DYLAN

Contents

1	The Beast Returns	1
2	Back from the Dead	16
3	The Rescue Party	28
4	All That is Holy	34
5	Fire and Stone	46
6	Celebrations	57
7	Beastly Familiars	63
8	Crow Bird	75
9	Bibles and Banishing	82
10	Puppy Love	92
11	Sneaking Suspicion	102
12	Hag Stones and Retrogrades	111
13	A Blast from the Past	123
14	Flatulence and Feathers	133
15	Frozen Stiff	147
16	On the Cards	158
17	The Great Escape	170
18	Goddess Talk	182
19	Secrets and Sorcery	195
20	In the Bag	207
21	Into the Cauldron	215
	Afterword	229
	About the Author	230

1

The Beast Returns

It was back.

Minerva woke in a cold sweat in the dark. She thought these things were supposed to skip a generation, but no, not this time. Fumbling for the light switch, she found it and turned it on.

'Oh Christ!' huffed a bleary eyed David before turning over and taking most of the duvet with him.

'It's back!' groaned Minerva, leaping out of bed, 'How bloody dare it!'

'What are you talking about?' said a muffled voice from the other side of the bed.

'I knew it,' said Minerva through gritted teeth, 'she's not been dead five minutes and she's sending me her left-overs. Well it can damn well bugger off back to where it came from. I don't want the bastard thing!'

David turned over with a groan. 'What thing?'

'The Black Dog. She's sent it, I just know it.'

David was sitting up in bed and rubbing his eyes. 'Who's she and how do you know?'

'*She* is my mother, and I *know* because I lived all my childhood with that beast in the house. It was my mother's companion and hardly ever left her side except for one time when she was almost but not quite happy if you know what I mean...'

David didn't know what she meant at all.

'It's a long story,' said Minerva, 'but the point is, my mother is no longer here and I thought she'd taken it with her, but no...'

'Have you actually seen it?' said David, searching for the crucifix around his neck. 'It sounds like a bad dream if you ask me. These things happen, Minerva.'

'When it concerns me and my family, I can tell you David, it's the real thing. Dreams can be a portal for these happenings, but that's not to say it isn't real.'

'Oh come on now...' David patted the empty space beside him and ran a hand through his hair. He wasn't up to a discussion on the meaning of reality at this unearthly time of day although with Minerva anything was possible.

'David, I do not need pacifying or patronizing so please spare me both. I'm telling you, the Black Dog has arrived, courtesy of my mother, and you'd better get used to it.'

'What, exactly do I have to get used to?' said David straining his eyes in the dim light.

'You won't catch sight of him, he's too cute for that,' said Minerva, getting back into bed.

David was stroking the point of his goatee beard like he always did when he was in deep thought. 'Are you telling me this Black Dog is invisible, that he can't be seen by the naked eye?'

'Yes I am and no he can't.'

'So his presence is something you sense more than anything

else?'

'Oh absolutely,' Minerva pulled the duvet up to her chin, 'I didn't spend all those teenage years with my mother and not get to know when he was about. And this is the worrying thing David…he was my mother's companion, not mine. And now he's here, just waiting for an opportunity to get under my skin. Can't you feel that dark energy?'

'Well it's certainly dark in here, which is hardly surprising at this hour. But no, I can't say I can sense anything else, although that's not to say it's not real. It quite obviously is to you.'

This is what she loved about David, he was so understanding. And it wasn't just because he was a vicar. 'Thank you,' she said, sighing heavily and fixing her eyes on the ceiling. 'You always say the right things.'

'Do I?'

'Yes you do. This Black Dog isn't the most believable of things is it?'

'Well no, but I have every faith in you and your ability to perceive the unbelievable. And I'm sure it's nothing that can't be worked out. You'll cope, you always do.'

'I hope you're right David, really I do. The Black Dog is a grim force of nature and I don't know that I'm up for a battle with him, because that's what it'll be. Are you ready for that? Can you put up with him?'

'You're talking as if he's come between us already. Is he really such a threat?'

Minerva clenched her jaw, 'You don't know what he's capable of, David. The dark night of the soul is upon me, I can feel it in the air and every cell of my body… he's getting under my skin already.'

'There's only one thing for it then,' sighed David, slipping his arm around her, 'how about getting under the covers? Something to take your mind off it.'

'There you go again, saying all the right things.'

'Hmm,' he said, nuzzling her neck, 'it's more a case of doing than saying.'

Minerva laughed and for a moment the Black Dog retreated into the dim shadows cast by a moon almost full and looming through the bedroom window. David's godly charms had overpowered the beast and its menacing presence. She would blot out its sinister energy by throwing herself fully into everything she knew to be good and opposite.

Giving herself to the moment and David, she harnessed the primal energy between them and sent it out into the ether. Their combined energies would protect her for long enough before the grisly intruder regained its strength and showed up again. In the meantime she needed to put it out of her mind and sex was the perfect distraction. She couldn't think of a better way to banish the creature for a while than pure, unadulterated love making.

* * *

Ronnie stopped off at the animal wholesalers to get more food. It was a trip she was making more often as the weeks went by...the puppies were costing a fortune to feed.

'Ron!'

Ronnie swung around from the sacks of puppy meal to see her old friend beaming at her. 'Hey Sophia! How're you doing?'

As she hugged her friend, Ronnie caught the unmistakable scent of horse.

'Just popped in for supplies…' said Sophia holding up a head collar, 'How about you?'

'The pups are eating for England. Honestly Sophia, you wouldn't believe how much they consume for the size of them!'

Sophia laughed, 'How old are they now? They'd just arrived when I last saw you.'

'Six weeks! Only another couple and they'll be off our hands…as long as it all goes according to plan.'

'Which is?'

'We get enough people wanting to buy them! You must come round and see them Sophia, they're really quite gorgeous.'

Ronnie flicked through her phone to find the latest photos of the pups. Bundles of black and white Springer Spaniels flashed across the screen as she watched Sophia's expression turn from surprise to delight.

'Oh my god, I'm going to have to come over…but don't let me have one will you? I've got enough on my plate with a bloody horse never mind a dog!'

'Don't hold me responsible for any weaknesses which may just show themselves when you see this motley crew…' said Ronnie with a grin, 'I'll warn you now, puppy power is a force to be reckoned with! Anyway, what about Diana? Wouldn't she just love a dog? You're still together aren't you?'

'Di moved in last week actually, so yes, we're very much together. It's brilliant Ron…never thought I could be so happy – but I am. And so is Di.'

'I'm pleased for you…bring her round too, it'd be nice to get to know her a bit better. Is she into dogs?'

Sophia laughed out loud, 'Oh she loves them. Hardly surprising as she's a vet now… just finished her final year.' She paused before taking on a serious look, 'Actually, it's her birthday in a few weeks time and come to think of it...oh god, you've got me going now!'

'Sounds like perfect timing,' said Ronnie with a huge grin, 'and the perfect present...winning combination if you ask me. And a vet? You're set for life there!'

'You're the devil in disguise, Rhiannon.'

'Me? Never! But wait till you see the pups...'

'They look positively angelic to me, but I can imagine what a handful they are, especially on a boat. It's not as if there's a lot of space is there? How are you coping with that?'

'Only just, as you'll see when you pop round,' said Ronnie, 'They've taken over, literally. Morrigan loves it of course, and how she's going to react when they go, I don't know...'

'You're not keeping any?'

'Not if I can help it, but then there's Joe...so it could be dangerous.'

Sophia smiled. 'Keeps you on your toes, eh? And my guess is, you love every minute of it if I know you...'

'Yeah, you're right...it's all a bit mad, but that's my life. Wouldn't have it any other way! I mean who'd live on a boat with a toddler, a half man - half pirate and eight dogs? Not forgetting Ropey of course, he comes with the territory.'

'I thought he was dead.'

'He is. But I can tell you he's very much alive in spirit and a frequent visitor. I have many a lively conversation with the old boy. It's all very friendly.'

'And not creepy? Jesus, I'd be crapping myself if I knew that there was a ghost on board. But then you're different, Ron...'

'Well, it all feels quite natural to me to be honest. I've had some strange but magical stuff happening for a while now. Ever since Bob...'

She looked down at the floor and shuffled her feet.

'Yeah I know Ron. It was hard losing him but look what you gained...a beautiful daughter and let's face it, Joe's stepped up to the role of a good provider for you both hasn't he?'

'Sometimes I have to pinch myself hard these days, for sure,' said Ronnie before glancing at her phone, 'Bugger, I've got to get back. I need to call in at Mum's on the way home...'

'How's she doing after your gran's death?'

'As mad as ever...but brilliant with Morrigan. And I'm hoping she'll have a puppy too although she's convinced at the moment she has enough on her plate with a Black Dog who seems to have attached itself to her.'

Sophia frowned. 'Really?'

'Really.'

Ronnie grabbed a large sack of puppy meal from a wooden pallet and kissed her friend on the cheek, 'Come round and we can catch up properly...text me when you're coming!'

'You're on, my friend. See you very soon!'

Ronnie made her purchase quickly before diving out of the shop and into the old Land Rover. She couldn't leave the pups for too long so it had to be a quick stop at Crafty Cottage on the way. Her mother had sounded quite desperate when she last spoke to her. This Black Dog wasn't going away any time soon by the sound of it, but like most issues concerning her mother, it was probably not quite as bad as she made out. Her mother did have a habit of blowing things out of proportion at times. But Ronnie could usually calm her down, as long as she got there before her mother had got to the brandy.

* * *

Isis couldn't wait to tell Minerva her news.

Singing completely out of tune, she bounced along the pavement, every step bringing her closer to Crafty cottage. She'd waited a long time to feel like this; in fact she never thought she *could* feel like this. This sort of happiness was the kind that belonged to other people, not Isis. But now it was right there in front of her - she could reach out and touch it - and she wasn't going to let it escape. Nothing was going to spoil it.

The first thing she noticed as she crept up the path was the music blasting out at high volume. It reminded her of Uncle Jasper's funeral a few years ago…she'd never forgotten it. One of those soggy tissues stuffed into handbags affairs with poor Aunt Ida collapsing outside as the coffin made its way to the cemetery, followed by the rest of the mourners. Why they played that depressing music she'd never understood, it only made people worse. Wasn't it enough to know someone had died without rubbing salt into the wound?

People are strange, thought Isis.

She wasn't surprised when there was no answer at the front door and for a moment stood there, wondering what to do. Minerva was obviously in, but clearly deaf to anything else. Not to be put off, Isis knocked harder at the door and was just about to make her way round to the back garden when a dark shadow appeared at the frosted glass.

At first, she didn't recognize who it was. The shadowy figure stood before her, bent over like a dying flower. Isis stepped back for a moment as the door opened wider and the dark figure disappeared behind it. What frightened her more than anything was the eerie silence in place of the thundering music.

She took a deep breath, 'Is that you, Minerva?'

'Can't you tell?' said the shadow.

Isis swallowed and tried to ignore the fluttering in her chest, 'Actually no, I can't. You're in the dark…literally.'

'That's because it's black and it's here.'

Isis began to rub her clammy hands together, '*What* is here, Minerva?'

'You can't see it?'

'No, I can't see anything.'

The hall light flickered on as Isis peered at the shadow taking form in front of her.

'Sorry, but I'm not sure what I'm supposed to be seeing…is it invisible?'

'You might be right, I had quite forgotten about my earlier life with my mother and the damn thing. I don't think I ever did see it.'

'Minerva, can you please tell me *what* you're talking about?' *She had been so excited.*

Minerva disappeared into the front room and slumped heavily onto the sofa while Isis followed and perched on the end of the sofa, watching her.

'It's been following me round for days and it has me in the palm of its paw, dreadful beast of a thing. I can't believe you don't see it but I'm telling you it's here, sat right at my feet now…'

She stared at her feet and so did Isis. 'Whatever it is Minerva, it's obviously very powerful…to have this affect. I've never seen you so dis-empowered. You're a shadow of your former self. Is it an animal, this beast of a thing?'

'Animal is far too good a description…' said Minerva, staring into space.

'Is it black?'

'Of course it's black. The colour of misery and despair is

never anything else is it?'

'I suppose not, but couldn't you imagine it's something else? A different colour...would that make it easier to put up with?'

Minerva's face darkened. 'Are you suggesting the Black Dog is in my imagination?'

'Well, yes , I suppose I am,' said Isis, quickly adding, 'but that's not to say it isn't real, Minerva. As you say so often yourself, just because we can't see something doesn't mean it isn't real. Believing is seeing, right? Not the other way round! Therefore, we can change it by thinking about it...that's how I've understood it. Perhaps I got it wrong...'

'No you haven't,' snapped Minerva, 'That is exactly right... the imagination is the doorway to all possibility...how could I forget?'

'Easily done when you're in the grips of such...fear. But fear isn't real is it?'

Isis squeezed her sweating hands together and clutched them close to her chest. It felt like her heart was about to leap out it was pounding so hard. She forced herself to stare at her feet and concentrated hard on her freshly painted toenails.

'I'd like to say I believe you Isis, really I would, but *this thing* has other ideas, I'm afraid.'

'And you're going to let it are you?'

'What do you mean?'

'You're going to let it control you? Have power over you? Is that what you want?'

Minerva turned slowly towards her, 'Isis, I do believe you have a point there...I mean, yes of course I remember what I have said in the past and it's absolutely right isn't it? Nothing has power over us unless we give it permission, unless we *allow* it to? The power always lies within ourselves...'

'That's what you've always told me Minerva and I must say, it's helped me out no end.'

'Do you think it would help if I focused on something else?'

'Absolutely,' said Isis glancing at the door, 'Something to take your mind off it.'

'I know just the thing,' said Minerva, getting up and making her way to the kitchen.

* * *

An hour and half a bottle of brandy later things were looking quite different.

'Is it still there?' said Isis, scanning the space around Minerva's body.

'Oh yes,' said Minerva, 'But nowhere near as prominent now, thank the Goddess.'

'Is it smaller now?'

'Yes. At least it was until you mentioned it,' groaned Minerva into her glass.

Isis caught her breath for a moment and felt for the ring on her left hand, 'I'm sorry, I shouldn't have! Anyway…I have something to tell you. Some good news!'

'Go on.'

Isis took another deep breath and looking straight at Minerva, held up her left hand and wiggled her ring finger towards her, beaming with delight.

'Is this some magical hand signal?' said Minerva, pouring herself another drink, 'Because if it is, I'm flummoxed. Would you care to spell it out?'

Isis laughed, 'I suppose in a way it IS a magical symbol, a symbol of our love…mine and Gerald's. We're getting married,

Minerva!'

'Good lord and lady'. She took another large gulp of brandy, fixing her gaze on the beaming Isis. 'When?'

'Last week.'

'You got married and never told me?'

'No. I said we were *getting* married, Minerva. We haven't done it yet!'

'Haven't you?'

Isis saw the wicked gleam in Minerva's eyes and felt the heat rising up her neck, 'Gerald *asked* me last week…to tie the knot with him, it's the real thing, Minerva!'

'You mean a handfasting?'

'It's a wedding isn't it?'

'Oh it most certainly is,' said Minerva quite seriously, 'None other than the most magical of *all* weddings. But is it legally binding?'

'It is in Dragonsbury, they do proper ceremonies and everything.'

'So that's where you're going? Dragonsbury?'

'I'm not sure yet. Gerald said he'd really like to get married in the woods, among the tree spirits and all of nature.'

'And not too many wasps I hope.'

'Not this time, no,' said Isis, 'That was such a shame wasn't it? Poor Gerald, he did suffer!'

'He did indeed. Perhaps we'll leave the bakewell tarts at home next time.'

'And I don't suppose rubbing one all over that piece of Willow had anything to do with it?!'

'That *piece of Willow*, Isis, was imbued with the magical summoning powers of sugar to do some very important work…bring back my libido if you remember correctly. And in true boomerang fashion, that's exactly what it did. It just so happened that Gerald in his wisdom, insisted on holding that particular ritual without a stitch on. Who could blame those wasps?'

'Yes, but he didn't ask for the boomerang to hit *him*!'

'Oh yes he did Isis, let's be honest,' said Minerva, finishing the last dregs from her glass.

Isis sat in silence, fiddling with her ringless finger, wondering what it would feel like when she had a ring to fiddle with.

Minerva sighed, 'Isis, I'm very happy for you, really I am. It's about time you had some real happiness and Gerald seems to be the one!'

'Do you think so?'

After a quick scan of the room Minerva picked up her trusty tarot cards from the mantelpiece. Taking her glasses beside them, she put them on and began to shuffle slowly and deliberately while Isis grew wide eyed and fidgety. Minerva picked a card and turned it over slowly. 'Five of cups, hmm…betrayal.'

Isis gasped, 'No it can't be…can it? Gerald wouldn't do that, he loves me!'

'No it's not Gerald,' said Minerva, confidently, 'Don't you see? It's Derek and it's in the past…I'm doing a three card spread here, past, present and future.'

She picked another card, laying it carefully next to Derek and his murky past.

Isis stared eagerly at the card, 'Well, if that's not Gerald I don't know who it is, do you?'

She let out a nervous giggle as her eyes skipped back and forth between the card and Minerva's face.

'I think you could be right there, Isis,' said Minerva picking up the card and holding it up like a grand prize, 'The King of Wands is one of the brightest sparks in the pack. And clearly...he holds a torch for you!'

She turned the card to Isis whose eyes gleamed as she looked at it.

It was undeniable. There in all his glory, was Gerald, carrying a torch, sitting on his throne and looking at her.

'Oh Minerva, how wonderful,' gushed Isis, 'It's all I could ever hope for, isn't it?'

'It's a good card - there's no denying it - and far out shadows the first one, yes, but...' she paused to gather her thoughts, 'one must be careful with such a magnetic character, he's a fiery sort and can burn easily and as much as he's warm and attractive and the life and soul of the party he can also be a chauvinistic so and so.' She peered over the top of her glasses to see Isis frowning.

'If I remember correctly, I seem to recall you using that very word to describe Derek!'

'I may well have done, but not quite in the same way Isis, you see...'

Isis didn't see.

'Oh Minerva he won't turn into another Derek will he? I couldn't stand it and then where would I be? Back where I started again!'

'Isis, stop panicking!' said Minerva, reaching for the brandy bottle, 'It is entirely possible to have two people with the same character traits and yet be quite different...and that's the point you see, the fact that Gerald is such a warm hearted individual and carries a torch for you far outweighs the chauvinistic side to him. It's obvious really.'

'Is it?'

'Yes, of course, it's just a warning. There are good and bad sides to every personality you know…we can't all be saints. It's a fact of life Isis and you might as well get used to it. The cards do not lie but one has to see them for what they are…'

'Which is?'

Minerva continued to shuffle the cards. 'They're just a guide, merely signposts along the road and it's *how* we interpret the signs which makes all the difference… sometimes it doesn't help to take them too seriously, that's all.'

'You said a three card spread. What's the third one?'

Isis watched in earnest as Minerva took her time shuffling and finally picked the last card. Silence fell upon the room, broken only by the ticking of the Green Man clock .

She smiled slowly as she turned over the last card, placing it next to the others on the black silk cloth. 'What more do you want than that?' she said triumphantly.

'Oh…the Queen of Wands!' shrieked Isis.

'Well I never,' said Minerva, 'if ever there was a match made in heaven, there it is. I can feel those fires of passion burning from here. If ever there was a woman for Gerald, it's you, Isis.'

'Do you think so?'

She clasped her hands together and held her breath.

'I'm telling you,' said Minerva, 'the tarot never lies.'

2

Back from the Dead

Ronnie stared at Joe over the sack of puppy meal. 'Say that again,' she whispered.

'There's a pony out on the marshes, skin and bone by all accounts and no one knows who it belongs to…seems to have appeared from nowhere.'

She felt her arms weaken as the heavy sack slid down her front and thudded onto the ground. 'Whereabouts on the marshes?'

'Near where those coloured ponies are, over by Rush's farm, on the headland beside that field…poor little thing it is…'

'You've seen it?'

'Yeah, I passed it today on the way back from Sloes – had to go and pick up some new overalls. It's only young I reckon, you know how you can tell. Proper lost looking it is…want to go and have a look?'

He watched her face flicker in front of him.

'Joe, what are you saying?'

'I only said did you want to see it? You might know someone out of all your horsey mates who might —'

'— Be able to rescue it? You know damn well what'll happen if I see it! We can't take on any more animals Joe…what with all the dogs and the pups and…'

'Whoa' there missus!' said Joe, 'Don't get ahead of yourself, I was only thinking of the poor little bugger, right sorry for itself it looks…'

As he puffed out swirls of smoke across the water, Ronnie shot past and back again, tossing the Land Rover keys at him. 'The pups are fed and Morrigan's staying on at nursery for an extra hour…come on!'

Joe grinned, 'Looks like you changed your mind then.'

She bounced onto the passenger seat as he climbed casually into the driver's side. 'I don't know what gives you that idea…' she murmured, staring firmly ahead.

* * *

Joe was right. Out there on the marshes, alone and cowering against the sharp wind, the small brown pony was a pitiful sight. Exposed to the open space of the surrounding fields he'd at least found some protection in a clump of Elders. He was huddled up close to them, his tiny head almost touching the ground when Ronnie caught a glimpse of a chain hanging from his scrawny neck, the heaviness of it weighing him down. It was as much as he could do to pit himself against it as his legs splayed out like a foal underneath him.

Her hand flew to her mouth, 'Oh Jesus!'

Joe pulled up as close to the headland as he could, by which time Ronnie was already out and running. Drawing the collar of his jacket high around his neck, he dug his hands deep into his pockets and followed her. He knew how much she still missed Bob, and although the dogs were good company and the pups great fun, nothing could take the place of horses, he guessed. They'd been her lifeblood for as long as he could remember...

Ronnie stopped and walked slowly towards the animal. 'I can't believe anyone would let something get this...bad.' She ran her hands over the coarse fur of his bony spine and looked under his belly.

'Well they did, someone did.'

'He's obviously been tethered somewhere...' she said, holding up the chain.

'Yeah, somewhere seriously lacking in any grass by the looks of it. I'm no expert on horses but it's bad, right? Is it a he or a she?'

'It's a he and he's not very old either, you were right...'

She very gently took the weight of the animal's head and parted the corner of his mouth and looked inside. 'I'd say no older than three or four at a guess'.

Her voice trailed off and she ran her hand down the matted clumps of fur on his scrawny neck. The animal leaned against her and sighed a heavy sigh. She continued to run the lightest of touches over his ribs, hidden only by fur and skin.

'Worms?' said Joe searching her face, 'Not surprising eh?'

Ronnie nodded and continued to run her hands deliberately over the animal. 'No, it's not and god knows what else is wrong...he's in a bad way. He needs help.'

She looked at Joe and he nodded, 'I'll ring Bill Rush and find out what he knows and we'll take it from there.'

'You'd better hurry, because he needs a vet and if no-one claims him...'

Joe touched her shoulder, 'Don't worry, he must be a tough little thing to survive out here...*somebody* must know who put him here, surely?'

He walked away tapping at his phone while Ronnie looked over the animal once more. She looked at his downcast eyes, dull like his coat, showing the faintest signs of life as he blinked and breathed warm air onto her hand in shallow breaths.

She couldn't leave him here, not now. He would die, that much was obvious. Out on the marshes at the start of winter, even the toughest of animals had a job to stay healthy...but one who was in such poor shape to begin with didn't stand a chance. She wanted to give him that. They had to help him.

Before she knew it, Joe was standing next to her. 'Bill says he doesn't know where the hell it came from or who's responsible but he's all set to come out and put it out of its misery...says it might be the kindest thing.'

'No he can't do that, Joe! Didn't you tell him?'

'I said we'd take him, but it'll have to be quick, Ron...do you know anyone who's got a trailer?'

She thought for a moment. 'I'll ring Sophia, she'll help. I know she will.'

'Get to it then - and correct me if I'm wrong - but time might not be on this little fella's side.'

'I know that.'

The wind whipped up and around them, cutting through the Elders and catching them all off guard. The pony stumbled towards Ronnie, falling onto his knees...and before she could stop him, he collapsed onto the hard ground.

She tried to pull him up by the chain, but it slid through her hands and as Joe grabbed hold of it she saw how shallow and quick the pony's breathing was.

'Joe...we need a vet, NOW. Ring Sophia! Her girlfriend's just qualified - she told me in the pet store - she might be able to give him something!'

'It'll need to be something good, that's for sure...maybe something to bring him back from the other side if we're not careful!'

Ronnie shot him a piercing look, 'Where there's life, there's hope, Joe.'

Kneeling down by the pony's head, she cradled it as gently as she could. 'You listen to me, little man,' she whispered against his hairy cheek. 'You're made of strong stuff, right?'

* * *

Minerva stared down at the smooth mound of earth and scattered lilies. 'I am not going to say it again, Mother, do you hear me?'

Why the silence surprised her so much was evident in her tight-lipped expression as she peered beneath the brown petals to the ground underneath. 'It may not be that long since you've been gone but I assume it's long enough to send that thing of yours over to do its work. Well, I'm telling you now, you can damn well take it back - I'm sure you must be missing it. You know how unhappy you always were without it, and yes, I know how much more unhappy you were when it was around but such is the nature of the beast. The Black Dog is *not* on my list of familiar companions thank you very much, so the sooner you remove his dark and dismal presence from my side, the better!'

Her hot breath billowed into the cold air and through the great Oak guarding her mother's grave. It was almost Samhain and the veil between the worlds grew thin, perfect conditions for magic.

She glanced nervously around, certain the dark shadow of a wolf-like creature was stalking her as she stood talking to her dead mother. I will not give in to it, she thought, as the wind whipped up around her legs, cutting through the thick woolly tights she'd struggled into earlier.

She reached for her hip flask and its warming contents. 'Look here, Mother,' she raised her voice in an attempt to sound braver than she felt, 'it seems you are hell bent on remaining as cold as the earth you're buried in, so I will bargain with you: How about I make an extra effort to tidy up the cottage and dispose of some of the more *magical* ornaments you despised so much? I'll get rid of my bone collection, especially the teeth from the shrunken head of a Nepalese postman and also the Ouija board you hated? Will that suffice? Is it a good enough deal for you to remove all traces of the Black Dog and his darkness from my side? What do you say?'

She waited as the late afternoon light merged with clouds and shadows, mustering up all kinds of shapes around the tree. And as the inky veil of night fell, she found comfort in the voice of the wind, the low hooting of an owl. And brandy.

She could hear laughter. *The old hag.* I might have known, thought Minerva.

'Right!' she shouted, 'I've given you a chance and it doesn't surprise me in the least that you've ignored me and why should it? True to form as per usual, Mother dear…that's the last time I come and try and make any sort of peace with you. Have it your own way, but mark my words, I will have mine too! And I know just the person who can help me… Aunt Crow returned that black beast to you before if you remember rightly? Not that anyone could blame him for leaving you in the first place, you were vile to him. But thanks to your beloved sister - who, if you recall, gave me the most educational as well as entertaining introduction to witchery – he beat a hasty retreat back to your loving arms after a particularly potent piece of magic. Aunt Crow always did know how to cast a good spell, *and* she was a better parent to me than you ever were!'

Minerva secured the lid of the hip flask and with head held high beat a hasty exit from her mother's graveside. Grappling in her bag for the keys to Mr. Morris she stumbled around to the passenger door and climbed across to the driver's seat - one day she *would* get that door fixed - but right now, she couldn't wait to get home, find Aunt Crow's number and call her.

She'd get rid of the Black Dog.

Aunt Crow might be eccentric, but a finer Witch you'd be hard pushed to find.

Checking the back seat for any unwanted passengers she turned the key while chanting the start-up spell which never failed:

'Hail Mr Morris! You must start...Bless your engine, bless your heart!'

The old car spluttered into life and faded out and died. She turned the key again, chanting loudly into the cold air rapidly forming a mist on the inside of the windscreen. Minerva chanted louder, twisting and turning the key urgently. What was the matter with Mr. Morris? He was prone to being temperamental but the magic always worked. She couldn't remember a time when it hadn't.

The temperature in the car was getting colder and the mist had crept onto all the windows, leaving nowhere visible at all. She was surrounded by the darkness of a typical winter's evening but it didn't feel typical to Minerva at all. It felt sinister and threatening and she wanted to go home. She wanted to get away from her mother's icy grip. She wanted to believe she'd gone when she'd slipped from this world to the next but something told her otherwise.

'Oh come on Mr. Morris, you *must* start! I demand it, this second!' she shouted at the walnut dashboard, 'Do *not* listen to my mother do you hear me?'

Minerva scanned the interior of the car which was icy cold now but the effect of it on her was quite the opposite: Small beads of sweat pricked at the back of her neck as her breath puffed out in shallow bursts. There it was again, a foreboding sense of misery which could easily have been her mother or the beast she'd sent to haunt her.

What if it was both? Minerva gasped as shadows flitted across the windscreen through the mist. She was trapped and helpless and completely overwhelmed by the oppressive air in the car. What if I'm dying? she thought. What if my time is done here and this is the final curtain? What now? Am I so insignificant and useless to the world that I must surrender to these dark and dismal forces? Is my light so dim that it bears no strength at all? She peered at the misty windscreen as a face appeared, blurred at first, but then it became clearer and she tried to blow on it but it was useless; her breath had no effect whatsoever and she froze.

She knew that face.

The lips were moving but there was no sound. The eyes were staring but there was no emotion. It was her mother and she was there right in front of her just inches away. Minerva blinked, unable to take her eyes off the grotesque image. This is a living nightmare, she thought, clenching her fists so hard the nails cut into her sweating palms.

The mouth on the face opened wider and the eyes narrowed and it rocked backwards and forwards as Minerva hung on tight to the steering wheel.

She's laughing at me.

'You can stop that, you Goddess forsaken hag!'

Minerva watched in horror as the face changed very slowly at first, into something not human. Her hands gripped tighter around the cold steering wheel and she held her breath while the image materialized in front of her. It was an animal, wolf-like, black and beastly. The Black Dog. How could she expect her mother to turn up without it?

Fear is a funny thing. A strange thing. More often than not it's the imagination gone mad. She'd told Ronnie many a time when she was little the same thing, and they'd pulled faces together and laughed until it had gone.

She didn't feel like laughing now, it wasn't one of those moments. But her mother thought so, she was making that quite clear. And the Black Dog, how dare it show up bold as brass, the bastard.

She'd never felt so helpless.

But there *was* somebody.

David would get her out of this awful predicament. 'Oh Mr. Morris, I'm so sorry you've had to witness this,' cried Minerva to the dashboard, 'but that's my mother for you I'm afraid. Never one for the subtleties in life!'

She patted the steering wheel and turned the key once again with renewed chanting. No response.

'I understand completely, Mr. Morris. It's been a shock hasn't it? Never mind, you'll need to get over it. We'll have you up and running in no time. I'll get Tilda Herd to come and sort you out, she's good with engines. It's that mechanical mind of his, I mean, *hers*.'

She tapped the steering wheel affectionately with one hand and reached for her phone with the other. When the light from the small screen flickered on, revealing the image of her mother again, she screamed.

'This is *not* happening,' said Minerva through gritted teeth, holding the phone right up to her mouth. 'By the Goddess of all that is holy and powerful, I command you, BE GONE!'

The image flashed on and off as the phone buzzed and made all kinds of strange noises before switching itself off. Minerva wished the eerie silence which followed would switch itself off but it didn't and she continued to stare at her phone, willing it to work with all her powers of manifestation.

David, she had to get hold of David.

Desperate, Minerva turned keys and pressed buttons until the phone eventually buzzed faintly back to life. She seized the moment and rang the vicarage, praying with every part of her being for David to be there.

'Minerva, is that you?'

'David, yes! Is that you?'

'Of course it's me. Who else would it be?'

'Are you sure you're not my mother or that thing in disguise?'

The silence deafened her, 'David, *David*, are you there?'

'Where are you, Minerva, and what's happened? You don't sound quite right.'

'That's because I'm not. I'm far from anywhere near it at the moment.'

'Where are you? The reception's bad and you sound very far away. You're not on the moon are you?'

'No such luck. I'm at the Field of Rest and strange things are happening, David.'

'At your mother's grave?'

'Yes, with Mr. Morris…but he won't start, not even with magic. There are dark forces at work David, I'm telling you.'

'And you think it's your mother?'

'I *know* it's her…and that demon dog.'

'Both of them?'

Minerva sighed. 'David, believe me, yes! Both of them are here or at least they have been…it was real. As real as we're speaking at the moment!'

'So the car won't start? I'll be there as soon as I can. Don't go anywhere.'

'There's no chance of that! I don't think I could get out of Mr. Morris if I tried.'

'Is the door stuck?'

'No. *I am*…it's paralyzing…and it's dark and they're *here* and I'm helpless to do anything. Believe me, I've tried!'

'Maybe you're trying too hard, Minerva. Nothing can harm you unless you allow it to. You're a strong woman.'

'I'm not feeling it at the moment David. She's bled me dry!'

'Are you breathing?'

'Of course I'm *breathing*. How would I be talking to you if I wasn't breathing?!'

'Exactly. You're alive with the blood pumping through your body. *She has not bled you dry.* No-one can do that unless you were back in the dark ages.'

'But that's what it feels like, David…evil forces like I have never felt before! Please don't tell me it's all in my mind because it isn't. My mother is here, her body may be cold and lifeless under those rotting lilies but her spirit roams free.

Don't you see? She has more independence now than ever and she is damn well making the most of it!'

The phone crackled, made a strange buzzing noise and David was gone. She had to believe the conversation had actually happened. She needed him.

Minerva focused every cell in her body on David. Apart from Ronnie, he was the only one who really understood her. The Goddess had brought them together.

She glanced at the rear view mirror and was almost as horrified to see herself instead of her mother, although at first it was hard to tell the difference. I'm losing myself, she thought, feeling more alone than ever. Grabbing the pentacle around her neck, she brought it to her lips and whispered:

'Bright Lady I call upon you now...for never have I been more in need of your help! Shine your light, lead me from this dark abyss where I cannot see an inch in front of myself. Lift this veil of fog! Take my mother and that awful beast away...please!'

She hung onto the steering wheel and pressed her forehead against the thin spokes and somehow it gave her comfort. She closed her eyes, because suddenly, she felt exhausted. Fixing her mind on the Goddess she began to feel a tingling in her fingers, creeping along her arms throughout the whole of her body. The current ran around her like a wave of energy, warming her, calming her...and she shifted her weight to welcome it.

Eventually, she opened her eyes and looked out of the driver's window. There, through the branches of the great Oak was the silver orb of an almost full moon rising. Sighing, she leaned back and gave a weak smile.

The Silver Lady had come. How could she ever doubt her?

3

The Rescue Party

Joe looked at Ronnie. 'You're the best chance he's got.'
'Me?'
She hardly recognized her own voice, it was so quiet.
'Yeah, you Ron. No better person for the job and besides, Morrigan will love him. You can teach her to ride, a proper little warrior queen we'll have on our hands!'

Ronnie swallowed hard and pushed the memories of Bob to the back of her mind. Three years had gone very quickly. A lifetime, in fact. Morrigan's lifetime.

'Well, he's standing now at least, and he needs to be able to handle the journey in a trailer. I'll try Sophia again, I'm pretty sure there's a stable just become available next to Kismet. If we can get him back to somewhere warm and dry, with good care – which I know I can give him – he stands a fighting chance. But it depends on what he's made of.'

Ronnie eventually managed to get through to Sophia. 'She's on her way with Diana *and* the trailer.'

'Nice one Ron. Let's hope it's not too late for this little bloke eh? I reckon he's a tough little thing to have got this far, don't you?'

'I'm not doubting that Joe, it just depends on how much damage has been done in the process. But he's a native, so yes, they're tough all right.'

'What else could be wrong?' said Joe, without taking his eyes off the wobbling pony. Ronnie slipped one hand around the underside of his neck and the other over his back, feeling the space between his ribs.

'Worm damage is the main issue, which could be lasting, but we'll see....' she pondered for a moment, 'You know, I'm pretty sure Sophia said that's how she met Diana. She came to give Kismet some vaccination and —'

'The horse wasn't the only one for a bit of treatment then...' Joe smirked, 'How about a roll in the hay with the vet afterwards?'

'Joe! I'm sure it wasn't like that at all. Why do you have to say things like that?'

'Oh come on Ron, I'm joking! I like Sophia, you know that. Any friend of yours is good enough for me, and to be honest – I couldn't give a toss whether she's with Arthur or Martha. People are people at the end of the day.'

'Exactly. And it will be very handy to have her opinion on this little chap...'

'He's in a bad way for sure'.

She hadn't heard him, 'What about Lazarus? I think it's the perfect name...'

Joe laughed softly, 'If that doesn't bring him back to life nothing will!'

She chewed her lip and looked at him.

'Don't worry Ron, we'll cope...we got a litter of pedigree pups to sell, remember. They'll fetch a good price, you know that.'

'Yes, I hadn't thought of that,' she glanced up at the sound of a vehicle rumbling towards them, 'And Sophia's having one, did I tell you?'

'What're you worrying about then? Everything works out in the end...'

'Let's hope it's not the end for this poor thing.'

'No I didn't mean that, you know I didn't, but he's in the lap of the gods now and it looks like we have two just showing up...or are they Goddesses? One of each perhaps?'

'Joe! Shut it please. Sophia's a good friend and I'm pleased she's found someone. Does anything else really matter?'

'Course it doesn't, Lazarus needs the good vibes, right?'

Joe's bright tones rang into the chilly night air as they watched the trailer backing up towards them, stopping just feet away. 'Good evening ladies! Compliments on the parking. Very impressive!'

Ronnie felt relief wash over her. For all his annoying habits at times, he was a charmer.

'Hey you two!' Sophia's melodic tones sang over the top of the vehicles. 'Yes Joe, practice makes perfect, eh? Don't sound so surprised, I've had enough of it in my time!'

'I don't doubt that one bit,' Joe pointed to Ronnie and smiled, 'You're as horse mad as this one...'

'It'll be good to be neighbours again, won't it Ron?' said Sophia, walking over to them.

Ronnie's eyes grew bigger, 'Is that stable really spare?'

'It is indeed,' said Sophia, 'Would you believe my neighbour sold her horse last week and it went today. She's giving up for some daft reason.'

Ronnie managed a smile, 'That's the magic at work, as Mum

would say!'

'Yes, you're right. Is this the patient?'

'Meet Lazarus,' said Joe, 'back from the dead and ready to rock.'

A second figure appeared from the back of the trailer, her tomboyish appearance complimenting the elegant Sophia.

'And *this* is Diana.'

'Pleased to meet you both,' said a quiet voice from under a baseball cap, 'In spite of the circumstances.'

'Nice to meet *you* Diana,' said Ronnie, 'And no, it's not the best situation—'

'But it's getting better all the time,' piped up Joe, 'Especially now you two are here. Great to meet you Diana.'

He extended a hand as he walked towards her and they shook hands.

Ronnie and Sophia swapped glances and smiled.

'Ever the charmer, Joe,' said Sophia, 'Which is why we love you so much of course!'

Diana walked quietly and confidently up to the pony, 'So who have we here, then?'

She ran her hands over his fragile body and producing a tiny torch, she shined the bright light into his eyes, gently pushing the eyelids back. After parting the corners of his mouth to look inside, she stepped back and lifted her baseball cap up, running loose strands of dark hair back into place before pulling the cap back down. 'He's very malnourished and will need a thorough worming programme, good food and a *lot* of care, but…'

Ronnie took a deep breath, 'Will he pull through? Do you think he stands a chance with the right care?'

Diana nodded slowly, 'If we can get him back to the yard, rug him up and get some good hay and alfalfa into him, he stands as good a chance as any. Sophia's told me how well you looked after your last horse so I'd say he's lucky you found him. Let's get him on board shall we?'

'I do like the sound of a good, strong woman,' said Joe, winking at Ronnie, 'And one who knows what she's talking about too. Much obliged, Diana.'

'It's a pleasure,' said Diana, smiling at Sophia. 'Glad to be of help.'

Soft laughter filled the night air and the four worked together to let down the ramp of the trailer while Ronnie took the head collar from Sophia and put it on Lazarus.

'It was the smallest I could find,' said Sophia as she watched Ronnie fastening up the buckles.

'It's fine, honestly,' said Ronnie, 'And a vast improvement on this thing…'

She held up the chain which Joe had managed to dismantle.

'Crikey, no wonder he's got no fur left with that weight around his neck,' said Sophia, 'Let's get him on board. Can you get behind him Joe and Di, while Ron and I take the front end?'

The four worked together and between them, almost carried the pony, who, apart from being as light as anything, put up no resistance at all.

'I'm staying here with him,' said Ronnie, one hand on his nose and the other around his neck. She felt him lean into her and bracing herself against the side of the trailer widened her stance to take the weight. As weak as he was, he was still a large animal.

'You sure you're okay in there Ron?' called Joe.

'Yes, fine,' she called out firmly, 'see you at the yard.'

She felt a shiver run down her spine and a strange sense of

something familiar standing beside her…somewhere between one world and the next. She knew that smell and saw him clearly in her mind. He was as close as Lazarus.

You didn't forget old friends and they didn't forget you. 'I'm so glad you're here,' she said under her breath, 'I need you Bob, now more than ever.'

4

All That is Holy

Minerva watched David from the front pew as he carefully arranged the candles on the altar. There were few things more attractive in a man than seeing him in his own working environment. And a vicar was no exception.

But unlike the rougher terrain of building sites and farmland where the rippling of male bodies fill the open spaces with raw testosterone - this was different. There was something about the inner sanctum of a holy place that heated up the Witch blood rising inside Minerva…and she surrendered to its giddy heights. However sacred or hallowed a space, there is no separating a Witch from her magic, or her man.

Fortunately, churches didn't unnerve her like they used to - she'd learnt to get over her hangovers from the dark ages - and she had David to be thankful for that. He was the perfect partner, putting her at ease in the most uncomfortable situations, which for one as magically inclined as Minerva, can't have been the easiest of things to do. But David did it very well indeed.

'I don't know what I'd do without you.'

David looked up, 'That's very sweet, what's brought this on?'

'If it hadn't been for you the other night, coming to my rescue, I'd still be stuck in Mr. Morris with my mother and the Black Dog prowling around.'

David raised his eyebrows, 'It's in the past Minerva, why not leave it there? Whatever happened the other night has been and gone.'

'Yes, I hear what you're saying,' said Minerva, glancing up at the stone walls and stained glass windows, 'I just wanted to say thank you for rescuing me, that's all.'

Without saying a word, David walked over to her and planted a soft kiss in the middle of her forehead. Sinking down on the hard wooden pew she savoured the warmth of his lips on her face. It was a pure baptism of fire.

He returned to the altar in silence and smiled at her. She could see the pale outline of an aura around his head and shoulders and felt the fluttering of angel wings in her stomach. Not here, not now, she thought, sitting up a little taller. 'Did I tell you about Isis…her *news*?'

'No, I don't think you did, I'm all ears,' said David, making a mental note to order more candles.

Minerva shuffled the pile of hymn books beside her and began to leaf through them one at a time, removing anything which shouldn't be there, 'Well you need to be because it's big news…*breaking*, as they say.'

'Do they?' said David, raising an eyebrow, 'In that case, you have my full attention.'

Minerva frowned in hesitation as she picked at a hard ball of chewing gum from the inside of a hymn book and placed it carefully onto a piece of tissue. 'They're tying the knot,' she said slowly and deliberately, 'Isis and Gerald.'

'When?' said David, his mind wandering already to the lengthy list of church engagements for the next twelve months, 'And where? Have they any ideas?'

'Possibly Dragonsbury, but Gerald fancies it in the woods at the back of his bungalow, according to Isis.'

David gave an abrupt cough as he lined up all the candles with the large silver crucifix in front of him, 'So they're not thinking of getting married here then?'

'Oh no,' said Minerva checking the tips of her fingers for any chewing gum remains, 'When I said tying the knot, I meant exactly that…a handfasting of course! A real Witch's wedding.'

'Isis isn't a Witch though, is she?' said David, stroking the silver candle holders with the church duster.

'No, not exactly,' said Minerva, 'Although we have talked about a dedication ritual to initiate her into the Craft – which will now be very much be on the cards I'd imagine – but no, I'm talking about Gerald. *He* is most certainly a Witch, although I was unconvinced to start with, I must admit. His manner *can* be a little overbearing at times and I don't much care for the domineering sort as you know.'

Yes, David did know.

He'd experienced enough conflict between Minerva and her domineering mother to last him a lifetime. Although he'd always found Cybele to be manageable, something happened between mother and daughter akin to any battlefield in history. Refereeing between two such volatile characters was a trying affair even for a man of his training, but he handled it with the utmost sensitivity, managing in the process to stay on the good side of both of them.

Ah now, you'd make a wonderful man of the cloth!

As his own mother would say, he had the knack of getting the best out of people. And he would often hear her Irish sing song cries echoing around the church walls as he pondered on the mysteries of his vocation.

'David!' said Minerva, 'Where have you gone?'

'Nowhere, I'm right here...'

'You've got that faraway look in your eyes, are you feeling all right?'

David straightened up and walked over to the front pew, 'I'm sorry,' he said, taking her hands in his, 'Forgive me, I was thinking about you and your mother, which reminded me of *my* mother and something I have to tell you... But first, please carry on with the news about Isis and Gerald.'

She smiled at him, enjoying the warmth of his hands on hers. 'There's not much more to tell. But yes, a handfasting, probably in the woods and I'm hoping they'll ask me to do it. Seems appropriate under the circumstances, don't you think? After all, I was the one who brought them together in Cordelia Nightshade's garden at the life art class.'

'Ah yes,' said David, turning to sit down beside her, 'You're quite the matchmaker, Minerva.'

She laughed, 'I don't set out to be, you know, these things tend to happen of their own accord to a certain extent. But magic does play a part without a doubt.'

David picked up a hymn book. 'Whatever or however these strange mysteries occur, it's a wonderful thing when two people come together, certainly.'

'You mean like we did?'

'In this very place if you remember correctly.'

She pondered for a moment. 'Three years is a long time ago David, it's a bit foggy I'm afraid.'

'I think the amount of brandy you'd had that evening might have been more to do with your fogginess than any length of time, Minerva.'

The light dancing in his eyes made her smile. 'Whichever way you look at it David, the memory is one of those things that can escape from one's grasp more easily than we think. That's why we're so good together, because what I forget, you somehow always remember. We're the perfect combination.'

Placing the hymn books to one side and taking Minerva's shoulders, he turned her towards him. 'True harmony,' he said, kissing her, 'is the balance of opposites.'

'The Goddess and the God you mean?'

'You could say that.'

'But is that what *you* think?' said Minerva in hushed tones, glancing across to the chapel dressing room.

He pulled her close to him and brushed her warm cheek with his own, whispering into the mass of red hair sticking to her neck, 'Have you ever had any reason to doubt me?'

'So far so good, is fair to say, I think,' said Minerva, feeling a shortness of breath and an urge to peel off the layers of clothes between them. 'Shouldn't we find somewhere more…private?'

'If you don't mind the choirboy robes and my collection of dog collars, we could retire to the dressing room over there,' said David, nuzzling the base of her neck.

'Retire is not quite what I had in mind,' said Minerva, 'More like recharge if you like.'

'I like the sound of that,' said David pulling her up slowly by the hand. 'What's a man to do with such a heavenly distraction in the workplace?'

She threw her red mane back and laughed. 'I'm waiting for you to show me,' she said, looking up at the domed roof above them. 'Will the boss mind?'

'There's no one more understanding,' he smiled. 'Human nature is after all, a heavenly thing.'

Their laughter echoed around the church and Minerva wondered if angels were as polite as people said they were - keeping themselves to themselves and only intervening in one's affairs if asked. She called out loud to Archangel Michael, shining in full technicolor glory beside the chapel dressing room, 'If you don't mind, Michael, I'd appreciate it if you could just stay where you are and keep guard. No waifs and strays for at least an hour please.'

Glancing up at the stained glass image, she was sure the angelic figure moved to get a better view of the pair as they entered the dressing room. 'You heard me Michael, stay where you are!' she growled under her breath as the silver shield glinted, and the rays of gold spun in all directions from his magnificent sword. 'You're the best bouncer in the building, now get on with the job!'

* * *

The smell of a freshly laid straw bed was something Ronnie didn't think she'd ever experience again. She breathed in deeply as she forked the golden straw up the sides and corners of the stable, making it as comfortable as possible for its new inhabitant. If Lazarus was going to be spending time laying down, he needed as much cushioning from a decent straw bed as possible.

The pony had practically fallen off the trailer when they arrived back at the yard, but had managed to keep his balance while he drank from the bucket of water offered to him. That was a good sign, at least he was drinking. The next thing was to tempt him with some food.

She opened the stable door and picked up the bucket of bran mash and gave it a final mix with her hand, turning over the dark, thick molasses into the warm and fluffy mixture. The sweet aroma filled the cold stable and she was pleased to see the slight twitching of a brown ear as she walked towards the dejected figure of Lazarus in the far corner.

'Here you are little man, something nice and tasty,' said Ronnie in a low, coaxing tone. 'It'll make you feel better.'

The pony turned away from the bucket and hung his head even lower.

'Not hungry then?'

Joe was leaning over the stable door, looking as tired as she felt.

'No.'

Ronnie gently stroked a shoulder bone sticking out sharply through the staring coat of brown fur and shot Joe a worried look.

'Give him time, eh Ron? He'll come round. He must be exhausted after all he's been through. You can't blame the poor old thing, but with a name like you've given him I reckon he'll be back on form in no time!'

His chirpy tone struck a dis-chord…she knew he was being brave for her.

'I'm staying with him.'

'I thought you might,' said Joe in a softer voice. 'I'll nip back and get you a sleeping bag…'

'Can you pick Morrigan up and —'

'— Sort the dogs out? Course I can,' said Joe. 'Don't worry, I can manage. All part of the service m'lady!'

He gave a half bow, winked and stuck a hand in the air as he turned and disappeared into the night. Quickly following came the familiar sound of the Land Rover coming to life and rumbling out of the yard. She peered out over the stable door, tracing the sound of voices to the light glowing under the tack room door.

It was good to know Sophia was there, but how strange it was to be back in the same part of the yard they'd shared when she had Bob. Standing there in his old stable, she breathed in the familiar earthy smells and smiled at the wheelbarrow propped against the red brick wall, a head collar hanging over its handles. She traced the tracks of its tyres on the muddy drive back to the steaming muck heap and felt a comforting sense of familiarity.

When Sophia and Diana appeared in the doorway of the tack room and walked slowly over to Ronnie, she thought how well they suited each other - Sophia's tall and willowy frame and the stocky and somewhat elusive Diana. This was a woman who didn't need anyone else and yet with Sophia, looked every inch the doting partner.

'How's he doing Ron?'

Sophia's grin turned to a look of concern.

'He won't eat, but he *is* drinking,' said Ronnie.

'And he's still standing, which is a good thing,' said Diana. 'Don't worry too much about the short feed at the moment if he won't touch it, as long as he's got good hay. Do you have any alfalfa?'

Ronnie shook her head, 'No, but I can get some tomorrow. I'm staying here with him tonight.'

'Good idea,' said Diana, 'the company will do him good. I'm guessing he's been on his own for a while.'

Sophia turned to her, 'How could anyone just leave an animal to fend for itself like that?'

'You'd be surprised how many would,' said Diana. 'But with good care and attention he stands every chance of pulling through and it looks like he's going to get it.' She smiled at Ronnie.

'Ron's the man for the job all right,' said Sophia. 'Great to have you back my friend! Anything we can get you? Food?'

Ronnie shook her head, 'No, but thanks anyway, Joe's bringing me back a sleeping bag and supplies, I'll be fine, honest.'

'Okay,' said Sophia and taking Diana's hand, turned to walk away, 'See you in the morning, bright and early!'

The morning seemed a long way off to Ronnie at that moment. She must get through the night first and with Lazarus looking so poorly she had to stay with him.

But she wasn't on her own.

Bob was there, it had been his stable after all. And if anyone could help her Bob could. If he'd come to take Lazarus, surely he wouldn't be so cruel to have brought her back here to do it?

Something made her jump. Her heart pounded at the munching coming from the corner of the stable and she looked across to the full hay net and watched as it began to bump gently away from the wall. But it wasn't Lazarus eating. From the other side of the stable he raised his head and turned towards the sound - she wasn't imagining it. Her whole body buzzed with a current of energy and feeling the tingling in her hands she reached out instantly to Lazarus, touching the matted fur and sinking down to the skin and bone of his emaciated form.

She placed both hands around his neck and ran them

along his back and up and down his legs, going where the energy directed them. Sometimes each hand would move in a different direction, massaging gently, stroking softly, holding still and skimming over until she stopped at his head. The pony pushed closer towards her and she held him between her hands, pulsing with a life force she trusted completely.

When the tears came, she didn't feel sad, but grateful.

The munching in the corner of the stable carried on and Lazarus rested fully against her while she stood quietly, not wanting to move. It was an odd sensation, as if something else had taken over and yet she was fully aware of herself and her surroundings.

As if waking from a dream she heard the chugging of the Land Rover coming into the yard, rumbling over the unmade drive. As the door slammed shut and footsteps approached she felt herself pulled from one world to another, as if she'd crossed a bridge and come back.

'How's it going?'

Joe's soft sing-song voice drifted towards her and she looked at him. The hazy glow around his head took her by surprise.

'What's up, you look like you've seen a ghost or something!'

'Maybe I have, or at least I heard one.'

'Well I can tell you, it wasn't me,' Joe pinched himself, 'Very much alive as you can see!'

'But that's the thing Joe, it sounded very much alive.'

'What? You mean you've just seen or heard something dead and yet it seemed alive? How come?'

'Oh I can't explain it Joe, but it happened anyway... like the time with Ropey and his cat and when I fell in the river... and when Gran died.'

'Yeah I remember. It's all happening again right? Well, it

only stands to reason doesn't it? Look at what's going on...you have an animal right here who's on death's door, why wouldn't it be happening? It's like you're at the same place again, in the same world.'

'It's more like *between* the worlds, Joe, but it doesn't scare me anymore. I'm kind of getting used to it.'

'Not a lot else you can do is there? You might as well accept that it's being given to you for a reason.'

'And like you've said before, best not to try and analyse it,' she said, whispering into the pony's mane, 'and just go with it.'

'Did I say that? I'm a wise old owl aren't I?'

She looked at his wavy brown hair catching the light from the stable.

'One in a million, Mum says.'

He chuckled softly, 'Now that's what I like about your mother, Ron, she says it how it is, every time. Ain't nothing like the truth, eh?'

'Did you bring the sleeping bag?'

'Sure did, and a flask and biscuits.'

'Is Morrigan okay? Did you call in and see her?'

Joe shook his head, 'No. Thought it best not to. I rang the childminder who didn't seem to mind at all, luckily. I don't suppose she would if she's getting paid extra would she?'

'Mary's very good,' said Ronnie. 'Morrigan loves being there with the cats and everything. She's got four!'

'Oh crikey, that'll be the next thing, a blinkin' kitten as well as a pony! That child is all set to be a zoo keeper when she's older I reckon.'

'Nothing wrong with that,' said Ronnie, 'She's only doing what comes naturally and copying us. It's not as if we try and discourage her is it?'

When Joe didn't answer, she peered over the stable door to see him walking towards the Land Rover, 'Wouldn't dream of it, she's a chip off the old block, Ron, just like her mother!'

There it was again…the bumping faster this time while the munching continued.

'I'm glad you think so too,' she said to the hay net, 'I really am.'

The night didn't seem so daunting now. It was comforting to know she had a good friend with her. What did it matter if he came from this world or the next?

5

Fire and Stone

Isis had looked in every room but couldn't find him anywhere.

Why hadn't she thought of the obvious place first? Walking faster through the kitchen and out of the back door, she was greeted by the naked figure of Herne the Hunter in the shrubbery. He was a fine specimen, reminding her of Gerald…that air of authority, the poise of power…but not just any kind of power. This figure had magic ingrained into every curvature, every knot in the golden wood, and as she stopped to study more closely she saw symbols swirling through the grain and over each body part. It was unique and remarkable, just like Gerald.

She reached out to touch the smoothness of the oak-stained figure when a voice from behind stopped her.

'Isis my love, what perfect synchronicity. Just in time to sample my latest creation.'

Gerald's words trickled over her like warm sunlight and closing her eyes, she fell into his embrace.

'And what would that be I wonder?' sighed Isis, not really

caring what it might be at all.

'I've been working on a ritual for Samhain of which part of it will be a dumb supper.'

'What's that? It sounds intriguing.'

'It's an ancient custom in honour of the dead, where our ancestors laid a place at the table for each family member beyond the veil.'

'Ah yes, that's what the festival's all about isn't it? The dead?'

'It's certainly a time of year when the veil is at its thinnest and most suitable for spirit work, yes,' said Gerald, taking her hand and leading her away from Herne to the small log cabin at the far end of the garden. 'I like to make the most of these cosmic tides and utilize the energy for magic of the deepest kind.'

'Oh,' said Isis, her hand pressed tight against her chest, 'I can feel it already Gerald.'

Gerald didn't say another word but led her in silence to the building where he tended his magical creations when he wasn't tending other people's gardens.

Inside the cabin, a small log burner glowed in the corner and thick plumes of earthy incense filled the air.

'What's that smell?' Isis wrinkled her nose, 'It's very strong.'

'Yes it needs to be,' said Gerald closing the door behind them, 'to imbue the space with the right elements for the work'

Isis nodded slowly, her gaze stopping at a bright coloured wall hanging. The gold thread sewn onto the dark magenta silk was familiar but she couldn't place the naked man at all. She could only think how uncomfortable he looked, his arms and legs stretched out wide to the edges of a circle.

It looked like Gerald. He had the same air of pure and simple manhood, a sense of dignified humanity - but she couldn't understand the odd position - especially without even a loin cloth to protect his modesty.

She glanced away quickly to find Gerald watching her closely. 'Do you know who that is, Isis?'

'I'm afraid I don't, but he looks familiar…'

Gerald laughed, his features becoming more serious as he walked over to the wall hanging and swung around to face her.

'This, my dear Isis, is one of Leonardo Da Vinci's greatest works - the Vitruvian Man - magically proportioned and proving himself to be the ideal microcosm, the perfect reflection of the divine macrocosm.'

Isis shuffled from one foot to another, 'And what would that be? I can't say I've ever heard those words before, Gerald.'

He rubbed his hands together, still tanned golden from the summer and she thought how wonderful those hands were. How caring and knowing they were, how *sensitive*.

He softened his look towards her, 'Simply speaking, Isis, it is the principle that there exists between man and the universe, a link - which we call a correspondence in magic – in which the macrocosm, which is the universe,' he pointed to the outer edges of the golden circle, 'is represented in miniature, here…' and pointing just below the centre of the naked image, 'in man and the microcosm.'

Isis turned a deep crimson. 'Oh yes, I see,' she said, blinking hard and loosening the silk scarf away from her neck, 'He reminds me of you Gerald!'

Gerald grew immediately taller and beamed at her, 'How very sweet of you Isis,' he said, puffing his chest out, 'I must say, I don't mind at all being likened to Leonardo's Vitruvian Man. He was rightly named, composed of earth, air, fire and water, just like the body of the planet itself.'

Isis watched as Gerald began to slowly undo the buttons of the green mohair cardigan she'd knitted for him. How it suited his olive skin, she thought, as the cardigan dropped to the floor. After peeling off his t-shirt, his hands moved to the brown corduroys of his muscular lower half and she gasped, 'You do this to me every time Gerald.'

'And what would that be my love?'

The words fell from his lips as the boxer shorts fell to the floor and all the while he didn't take his eyes off her. She was frozen to the spot and yet melting under his gaze.

I'm a mass of contradictions, thought Isis not really knowing where to look or what to think. Her breathing was coming in shallow gasps and she felt a heat creeping over her body in a series of delightful sensations. It had never been like this with Derek, but then Derek was not Gerald. She couldn't believe how different her disastrous marriage had been compared to what she had now with this man of magic and mystery.

'Gerald,' she said feverishly, 'The dumb supper... what was it you wanted to show me?'

Gerald laughed softly and stood in front of the wall hanging, looking just like the Vitruvian Man. The only thing he wore was a huge grin causing Isis to step back. He was on fire. Or rather, *she was.*

'Isis, behind you...the candle!'

But it was too late. It happened so quickly and all she could do was scream.

She remembered looking down and for a moment couldn't distinguish between the orange of her harem pants and the flames. She screamed again and stopped as the water hit her. Gerald stood, one arm raised in the air, pouring from the fish head vase. Not only was she soaking wet but covered in soggy leaves pricking her skin like needles. 'Gerald, I'm burning! Help!'

'Isis, no you're not! Keep still!' he shouted, 'It's the holly.'

'What?'

Isis felt the thin silk of her harem pants sticking to her skin and caught the leaves with her hands, 'Argh! Are you sure I'm not on fire?'

'You are NOT on fire, Isis!'

She could feel his hot breath on her face and turned away, to find the Vitruvian Man staring back. She turned back to Gerald's face, inches away from her own. 'I'm soaking wet!' she whined.

'But you're not burnt,' said Gerald scanning her dripping form. 'Thank the gods for my holly and ivy.'

'Oh that's what this is,' said Isis pulling the sodden heart-shaped leaves from her drooping hairpiece.

'A magic temple is not complete without the male and the female, it keeps everything in balance, Isis,' said Gerald picking up the prickly holly and ivy leaves and placing them together on the altar. 'One must pay homage to the Lord and the Lady!'

'Gerald, I'm soaking...'

'Oh my love!' he said, taking her in his arms, 'What a fright you've had. We must get you stripped down and dry you off by the stove.'

He peeled the wet clothes from her skin slowly and threw them into the corner by the door. Isis didn't care anymore, her nerves had suffered enough. She sank into his arms as he pulled her towards him, her body easing into his.

'I'm so glad you were here,' she sighed, 'I'm not sure what I'd have done if you hadn't been. You have a habit of being in the right place at the right time Gerald, you really do.'

He squeezed her against him, 'Isis, you need have no fear when I'm around. I am here to look after you, of that you can be sure.'

'Do you mean that?'

'I most certainly do,' said Gerald pressing his body hard against hers.

Isis let out a heavy sigh and looked up at the wall hanging as they slid down onto the shag pile rug. How wonderful to be loved. How marvelous to have this chance to be happy, although sad to realize that with Derek, she'd never been anywhere near it.

She thought she had. She thought they were together forever, but now, with Gerald she felt so far removed from that time in her life, it was as if it had happened to someone else. This was her time to discover who she really was.

'You have no idea what you've done Gerald…' she sighed, glancing up at the Vitruvian Man.

'Oh I think I do,' he said with a low chuckle, 'Trust me, my love, I do.'

* * *

Minerva looked up at the string of delicately carved cherubims hovering in the stone alcove above them. 'Hmmm,' she sighed, 'I know exactly how they feel, or at least I think I do.'

David quickly covered her with a choir boy's robe draped over the back of the small sofa where they sidled up close to each other. 'And how exactly is that?' said David, his eyes flitting from the discarded dog collar on the flagstone tiles to the beaming cherubs on the ceiling.

Minerva stared hard at the cherubs, 'I do believe they're the happiest little things I've seen in a long time.'

He kissed her glowing cheeks. 'I'm glad about that,' he sighed, 'And their joy is positively contagious, just like you.'

'I'm not sure how I feel about that, the *plague* was contagious,' said Minerva, her eyes wandering to the large, silver crucifix in the corner of the room.

'Not even a joyous one?' said David, 'I can't think of a better way to spend my days than being plagued by your irresistible charms.'

She laughed, scanning the floor for any hastily discarded underwear, 'I shall remind you of that when the Black Dog chooses to plague me again.'

He breathed into the red hair caught between them in clumps, 'Enough of that,' he said, pushing a slim white finger to her lips, 'It's not the sort of pillow talk that'll get you anywhere.'

'Won't it?'

'You know very well it won't. Let's concentrate instead on the more positive influences,' he looked up at the cherubs, 'like the sweet music of the spheres.'

'Yes, I suppose the tinkling of the odd harp or two is preferable to the clash of heavy metal and impending doom.'

They laughed together and after what seemed like an age, Minerva pulled away from David's arms to look him straight in the eye, 'Your mother. What were you going to tell me?'

He took a deep breath, 'Ah yes, my mother…'

She began to dress quickly without looking at him, 'You said you had something to tell me about your mother, what is it?'

David cleared his throat, 'Er yes, she's coming over…to visit.'

The woollen tights stopped at her knees as Minerva paused to look at him, 'When?'

'Well, she's talking about coming over for All Souls…she still misses my father and wants to see me. Only natural I suppose.'

'How long since —?'

'Oh, almost ten years now…' said David picking up the dog collar and putting it back on before anything else. 'And on the 31st of October would you believe?'

Minerva stared at him, 'Your father died at Samhain? How magical, if I may say so…er, how did he —'

David quickly put on the rest of his clothes. 'An accident on the farm took him suddenly. Got caught up in a baling machine. It was a terrible shock, especially to Mother, she never got over it.'

Minerva's hands flew to her mouth, 'Oh David, how awful for you and for your mother, for *all* of you. At least she has your sisters close by doesn't she?'

David nodded, 'Annie and Charlene run the dairy side of things and their husbands work the land. Yes, it's a great comfort knowing they all keep an eye on her. They're only next door which is handy.'

'Yes, how reassuring,' said Minerva chewing her bottom lip, 'Of course she must miss you and especially at this time of year. I shall look forward to meeting her.'

David gave a small cough, 'I'm sure we can organize that Minerva, but she *is* rather opinionated, and a Catholic. It does seem to go with the territory.'

'Being Irish you mean?'

'In some ways, yes. There's a general rule of three to bear in mind when it comes to any conversation with my mother.'

Minerva bit her lip hard, 'Rules?'

'Er yes, three conversation topics which are off limits: Politics, religion and sex. If you can keep away from all three, you stand some kind of a chance with her.'

'And if not?'

David raised both eyebrows and hands to the heavens, 'I wouldn't advise it, let's put it that way, shall we? Forewarned is forearmed, Minerva. Don't goad her with any of those and you'll be fine.'

Minerva was quiet for a moment. She hated restrictions and normally didn't abide by any kind of rule – they always had the opposite effect on her - but in this case, she might have to conform for once.

'Well, as alien as that feels to someone like myself, I suppose I'd better take it on board, considering it's your mother we're talking about. When you say *religion*, what exactly do you mean?'

She scrunched her red mane into a velvet band and pulled it back from her face. Two bright green eyes flashed at him and David thought how like the Magdalene she looked. His mother would either love her or hate her.

'Perhaps it would be easier not to mention what you do, Minerva, to avoid any misunderstandings. My mother can be quick to judge, unfortunately.'

'If it's witchcraft you're referring to, what I *do* has nothing to do with religion. I have never been religious and I'm certainly not about to start now. As I've said before, you know only too well, the Craft is a reflection of not so much what I do but *who I am*. It's as natural to me as breathing, and to restrict me by rule and regulation is as good as any life sentence.'

Her hand flew to her neck and she could feel the beginnings of a hot flush creeping its way up her spine.

'Minerva, I think you're getting ahead of yourself,' said David with a sigh, 'No one is condemning you for your beliefs!'

'You say that David, but your mother being *Catholic* is bound to think otherwise wouldn't you say? Spawn of the devil is something I have been labelled with on more than one occasion!'

'Calm down Minerva, she's not even here yet, and who's doing the judging now? All I'm saying is, perhaps just refraining from being quite so obviously *witchy* might be the best option with my mother – for the sake of peace. Is that too much to ask for? I don't expect you to be anyone other than you, just a diluted version maybe? It'll only be for a few days, she won't be staying long.'

He was dressed and standing in front of her, inviting her towards him with open arms and that magnetic smile. As much as she wanted to resist, it was no good. She fell against his chest and sighed, 'David, please don't ask me to not be who I am. Not you, I couldn't bear it.'

'I'm not, at all,' he whispered, 'I know my mother, Minerva, and I want her to like you, which I'm sure she will, but just don't *say* you're a Witch, while she's here. It will make both our lives easier, believe me.'

She wanted to believe him, she really did. But there was something about his mother's impending visit that unnerved her and out of the corner of her eye she caught a glimmer of a dark shape passing. And that smell, what was it? She'd smelt it many a time out in the woods...the scent of something dead. A wild animal.

How foolish to think it was gone. And even more foolish to think it wouldn't come back. I won't say a word, she thought. David had more than enough on his plate but then who would exorcise the beast? She'd got him in mind for the job but then maybe she just ought to do it herself. After all, wasn't that the beauty of magical power?

The gold crucifix around David's neck glinting in the early afternoon light planted a seed in her mind and she smiled at him, 'David, have no fear. I promise I shall be on my best behaviour for your mother's visit.'

'I'm glad to hear it. Oh and one more thing I forgot to mention,' said David busying himself with boxes of candles, 'She's tee-total, my mother, so it might be wise to —'

'— Dilute that area too? Why of course,' said Minerva, making a mental note to check up on her stock of brandy when she got home. 'Already I can feel the nurturing influence of your mother around me…it won't do me any harm at all.'

'I knew you'd understand,' said David, with a look of admiration.

She kissed the small area of skin between the dog collar and the back of his ear, 'When have I given you any reason to doubt me, vicar?'

David chuckled as the chapel door creaked open and Minerva marched out, sending a silent prayer behind her.

6

Celebrations

Ronnie pulled up outside the Old Druid and leapt out of the Land Rover. Smoothing her dark hair back from her face, she bolted inside and within seconds she was standing next to Joe at the bar.

'Blimey, where did you come from?' said Joe, signalling to Ernie for more drinks.

'Where do you think?' said a wide eyed Ronnie, kissing him.

'Thought I recognized the smell of horse. How is the little fella?'

'Joe, you won't believe it, he's drinking and he managed half of a bowl of hot mash earlier and I've just filled the hay net *again!*'

'That's great news, Ron. Lazarus, living up to his name eh?'

'You were the one who was so sure he'd pull through.'

'I had a feeling, yeah. I reckon this is a cause for celebration don't you? What're you drinking?'

Ronnie looked at the large clock between the rack of spirits, 'I said I'd pick Morrigan up at seven, so...'

'Where from?'

'She's at Mum's at the moment. I suppose I could have one, couldn't I?'

'You surely could,' said Joe, tapping the bar for Ernie's attention. 'Another Druid fluid please, Ern.'

Ronnie grabbed Joe's arm with both hands and pulled herself towards him. 'Thank you, kind sir.'

'The pleasure's all mine m'lady, you deserve it. You've nursed him back to health good and proper by the sounds of it…almost worth spending the last few nights in bed alone for!'

She grinned as he passed her a tall glass of frothy golden fluid. 'That's what I've missed more than anything, that lovely smile of yours. Don't like seeing you worried Ron, it doesn't suit you.'

'No, I can't say I enjoy it much either,' she stopped to take a long mouthful of her drink, 'But you know what, I started to feel differently once I'd got the signal from Bob.'

Joe peered at her over the top of his glass, 'Go on…'

'I wasn't entirely sure myself how things were going to go, but that first night when we brought him back from the marshes…it sounds daft but…'

'When have I ever said that?'

'How about when I told you I saw Ropey's dead cat and then fell in the water?'

'Well, you have to admit that was pretty unreal, even for me to get my head round. It's not everyday your girlfriend has a near death experience is it?'

'No, but the truth is, it happened and I *know* what I saw. Anyway, in the stable that first night with Lazarus, the hay net started bumping up and down on the wall, *by itself.*'

'Say that again?'

As Ronnie repeated herself he took a long drink from his

glass. 'And you're saying that was Bob, back from the dead?'

'Joe, there is no *back from the dead*. I don't really think anyone or anything disappears completely. They move on to another world yes, but it's not a dead world – not in my experience anyway – it's very much alive. *They* are still alive, just in a different place, that's all. And I just know that was Bob...who or what else could it have been?'

Joe scratched his head, 'You really got me there, Ron.' This was followed by a quick burst into song...and Joe's version of the old Kinks hit.

Ronnie was laughing and punching him at the same time. 'Joe, p*lease!* I'm being serious.'

Joe grabbed her and coaxed her into dancing around the tables in front of the bar until they collapsed onto a bench by the fireplace. 'A little bit of dancing does you good, but it doesn't mean I don't take what you say seriously, course I do.'

She knew what he meant. It was only a few years ago his mum had died, and she knew the wound was still raw - but this was how Joe dealt with it – he joked.

'I'm not asking you to believe me, Joe, just understand, that's all,' said Ronnie quietly.

'Yeah, I know. But the funny thing is, I *want* to believe you. Maybe if I saw and felt what *you* do, it would be easier.' His voice was almost a whisper, 'If that's really Bob around, then power to him. He's doing an awesome job. And I suppose if people can communicate from that world, like you say, then why wouldn't an animal? It makes sense to me.'

Ronnie nodded and drank deeply from her glass, 'I'm glad you understand...it helps, it really does.'

They slipped into silence as the soulful sounds of Motown came bursting from the old jukebox in the corner. Joe tapped the side of his glass with his fingers and turned to her with a cheeky grin, 'Talking of understanding, I've got some news.'

'What kind of *news?*'

He shuffled around on the bar stool and looked into his glass, 'Band news.'

Ronnie knew how much Joe loved his band, 'Oh?' she said, downing her drink.

'Stag's gotta go. His drumming's just not been up to scratch these last few gigs. You know how you can tell when someone doesn't have their heart in it anymore?'

She nodded and noticed how his leg twitched in time with his fingers.

'Yeah, shame really, he's been with us from the start and I'm not sure what's going on but he won't talk about it. I've tried. So there's the end of a chapter. Anyway, the good news is, as luck would have it, I met a guy at work the other day– and it turns out he's a drummer. Well, we got chatting and he's coming over tomorrow for a session with us, and he's popping in tonight for a drink first.'

'Tonight?'

'Yep,' Joe looked up at the clock, 'any time now I reckon. Nice bloke, you'll like him, he's quite a character.'

Ronnie felt a twinge of something in her gut. 'I look forward to meeting him.'

'He'll be here soon…only lives a stone throw away in Northminster, which'll be handy for rehearsals and gigs.'

'Sounds great,' said Ronnie, 'But I can't stay Joe, I must go and get Morrigan. As much as she loves being with Mum, she does tend to get pretty wired when she's there. And afterwards it always takes a while for her to calm down enough to even *want* to go to bed, let alone, sleep.'

Joe laughed, 'Yeah well, your mother seems to have that effect on a lot of people Ron. Must be that magical stuff she's into…get's into the bloodstream and does all sorts of weird and wonderful things!'

'That's right,' laughed Ronnie, pointing to the crumpled packet of tobacco bulging from his pocket, 'You'd know about weird and wonderful stuff in the bloodstream wouldn't you?!'

'Well there's the voice of pure innocence if ever I heard one. Don't tell me you haven't enjoyed the odd spliff now and then!'

'Yes, alright it has been known, but I don't have your stamina in that department, Joe. I don't know how you do it sometimes.'

'Ron, I told you a thousand times, you're exaggerating! Nothing wrong with a herbal supplement to chill out with now and again. It's not as if I'm always on it and I don't smoke at work, you know that. Only in my own time and when I'm with the band, which is traditional, as you know.'

'I just worry sometimes, that's all.'

'You don't need to! Give me some credit Ron, it's not as if I'm on the hard stuff is it? I've never missed a day off work and I look after you and Morrigan all right don't I?'

'I'm sorry,' she touched his hand, 'I'll leave you to it. Looks like you have company anyway.'

They looked across to the far side of the bar as the door slammed heavily behind a blur of bright orange. The tall figure in a high viz jacket bounced over to them, thrusting his hand towards Joe, 'Hey mate!'

'Glad you could make it Allan,' said Joe, 'This is my good woman and Ronnie, this is —'

' — Allan Key at your service madam. And the pleasure is all mine!'

He took her hand to kiss it and Ronnie managed a half smile.

'Pleased to meet you Allan, you're a drummer I hear!'

He thrust his orange chest out, 'I am indeed, Ronnie! Is that short for Ronata?'

'Rhiannon actually,' said Joe, gesturing to Ernie for more drinks.

'Rhiannon! One of my favourite Fleetwood Mac numbers, *and* a Goddess I believe?'

'That's correct,' said Ronnie, glancing up at the clock as she edged her way towards the door. 'I don't mean to be rude but I must go, I need to be somewhere.'

'Then you must be gone!' boomed Allan, taking a bow.

Joe stood up and caught her hand, 'See you later, I won't be too long.'

'You take as long as you want,' she called behind her, 'Looks like you have a lot to talk about!'

As the door slammed behind her, Joe and Allan exchanged looks.

'Seems like you have a good lady there…'

Joe reached for his tobacco pouch, 'You're right, and like good drummers they don't come around too often.' He pointed outside to the beer garden, 'Shall we?'

7

Beastly Familiars

Ronnie stared out of the back door to where her mother was pointing. There, sitting on the stump of the old cherry tree was Morrigan; legs banging, hands clapping, and squealing with joy.

'What's she seen?' said Ronnie, peering at the twinkling lights at the bottom of the garden.

A loud squawk and a flapping of wings stopped Minerva before she had a chance to reply. 'Do you see it?' she said softly.

'Is it a crow?'

'And why wouldn't it be? Only to be expected don't you think?'

Ronnie could just make out the shape of a bird on the grass in front of her daughter. It was nodding and hopping back and forth around the stump as Morrigan whooped with delight, beating her tiny hands together and hammering the stump with her feet. This seemed to encourage the squawking bird as it hopped in time to the toddler's movements.

'It's dancing,' chuckled Ronnie.

'And she's talking,' said Minerva, 'she's *communicating* with the bird and it's talking back! She's doing just what I thought she would.'

'Which is?'

'She's growing into that name of hers right in front of our eyes! I told you at the time you named her if you remember. There's tremendous power in a name Rhiannon, you know that! And your daughter is living proof of the magic at work. And now that bird, what more evidence do you need? There is the warrior queen Goddess in our midst, speaking to us through her namesake and power animal. There's no denying it!'

Ronnie sighed, 'Hmm, there's no doubt about it she does love animals and they seem to love her, especially the crows. Out on our walks, they literally flock towards her.'

'Well there you are then, nothing speaks louder than the magic of nature. All we have to do is listen to what it has to say.'

'So, apart from the obvious, what's going on here?' Ronnie pointed towards the toddler and the crow happily chatting away to each other, 'What's the *magical* meaning of it?'

Minerva turned away for a moment and returned with her red velvet bag of cards. 'Time for the tarot I think, come and sit down, Ron, and let's ask them. I've no doubt we shall receive just what we need from them, as always. Morrigan's fine out there, she's enjoying herself, and we can keep an eye on her…'

Sitting at the round table in her old home, Ronnie felt a sense of comfort. There were so many memories here and so much had happened in such a short space of time that she wondered what might be next and more importantly, if she could handle it. The cards did have an uncanny knack of shedding light on things while her mother reached for them as naturally as breathing. Witches couldn't help themselves.

Ronnie lit a candle while Minerva shuffled the cards slowly, taking a quiet moment to compose herself and clear her mind.

Turning over the first card, she smiled at it like an old friend. 'Well, you asked for a magical meaning and here is none other than the bearer of those very tidings – and one of my favourite cards – the Magician himself.'

'Meaning?' said Ronnie, peering past her mother at Morrigan and the crow.

'In short, he is the guide who helps us direct our power to achieve whatever we want. He helps to develop our skills into talents, create with confidence the *reality* of our dreams…and to actually make them happen.'

Ronnie looked at her mother, 'He makes dreams happen?'

'Only if we can focus that energy, the spiritual life force we all have, into action.'

She pointed at the Magician's raised hand, 'As above, so below Rhiannon. He takes the power of creation and literally grounds it into physical reality. But unless we learn how to use that power, our potential remains unfulfilled.'

'As within, so without…'

Minerva laughed, 'Yes, indeed, you remember well, dear daughter! It's up to us what we do with our own power, but first we must find it and some do that more easily than others. Some become aware very early on.' She gazed out through the back door at the toddler and the crow. 'And right there before our eyes is evidence of the Magician at work, albeit a miniature one at the moment, but she's no less powerful!'

Ronnie grinned at the squeals coming from the garden. 'Oh she knows what she wants all right, *and* usually gets it. She's certainly got an uncanny knack for it, but aren't most kids like that until they learn they can't have everything they want?'

'Yes, you've got a point,' said Minerva peering over her glasses at Ronnie, 'But on the other hand Morrigan isn't *most kids* either. She has a natural ability to make things happen, to create magic, and what's important, to communicate that to others. Look at her now,' she pointed at her granddaughter, 'if that's not the Magician at work, I don't know what is!'

They watched in awe at the spectacle in the garden until a shadow flitted behind Morrigan and the bird. There in the herb patch, perched on Hecate's shoulders, was Lucifer. The black cat and the black marble statue were difficult to separate in the darkness and at first glance one could be forgiven for believing they were one.

'Oh no,' hissed Ronnie, getting up, 'he's after the bird and knowing Lucifer, he's quite capable of getting it.'

Minerva signalled her to sit down again. 'Leave them,' she said quietly.

They watched closely as Morrigan turned towards Hecate and the cat perching precariously on her shoulders and screamed. It was a piercing sound, loud enough to serve as a warning to the crow who leapt from the grass onto the greenhouse roof, cawing loudly.

Lucifer, already poised for action and undeterred by the small and insignificant human, took no time in deciding the distance between himself and the crow was short enough to justify an attempt to reach him. He sprang immediately from the Goddess to the greenhouse and onto the flapping crow.

Morrigan ran towards them both, arms outstretched and screaming wildly. Ignoring her, Lucifer was instantly upon the bird, pinning him to the glass as the creature fought against his weight. Leaving the Magician to his own devices on the table, Minerva and Ronnie shot up and out into the garden.

'Lucifer, you murderous bastard!' Minerva screeched, 'Get off it! GET OFF IT!'

Ronnie grabbed the screaming Morrigan and swung her small body away from the greenhouse. But Morrigan fought against her, intent on remaining on the battlefield where she was needed. Small fists pounded on Ronnie's chest and cries of frustration wailed in her ears. 'Birdy! birdy! BIRDY!'

'Morrigan, stop it!'

The crash of shattering glass pierced through the wailing cries as lights flickered from the neighbouring houses. Without thinking, Minerva hurled herself at the cat and the crow who were now tussling on the grass. Ronnie hung onto her screaming daughter while her mother grabbed Lucifer by the scruff of his neck with one hand and the flapping crow with the other. Nobody was giving in without a fight and although cats pounce and birds fly, humans hang on and shake if they have to. Which is exactly what Minerva did, giving Lucifer no choice but to drop the bird. However, his parting shot as he hissed loudly at his human jailor, was to sink his claws into her exposed, warm flesh.

'Aargh!' cried Minerva, 'You wild bastard!'

In that second, knowing the prize was no longer his, Lucifer disappeared into the inky blackness of the night and over the back field to nurse his fallen pride. You might think that cats don't have those kind of feelings but Lucifer being an exception to the rule had plenty of them.

'Is there blood?'

Minerva lay face down on the wet grass, clutching the crow with both hands.

'I don't know, I can't see,' said Ronnie, 'Is it alive?'

'Just about, I think,' said Minerva inspecting the fluttering bird. 'I'm not sure about me though…'

Ronnie let the anxious toddler down to join her grandmother and the crow. 'Mum, come on, get up and let's get inside. Have you got a box or something to keep it in?'

'Yes,' said Minerva, 'Lucifer's pet carrier which we've never used. I bought it when he came home that time with his ear hanging off after a fight - but he ran off.'

'Yes, and if I remember correctly,' said Ronnie, 'You were looking for him for days after. But he came back eventually, with various battle scars and half an ear.'

'And now he's given *me* battle scars, the monster!'

She held her hands out to Morrigan who stroked the crow's damp feathers gently and pointed at the large gash on her grandmother's arm, oozing blood. 'Granny hurt,' she said pulling a face, 'Drink make it better?'

'Now there's a girl after my own heart,' said Minerva, 'I do believe you're talking about a certain medicinal beverage, which will certainly help to make it better. Shall we go in and find it and put Crow Bird to bed?'

The toddler jumped up and down beating her hands together, big brown eyes widening under a dark fringe. Minerva thought how black like the crow her hair was and there was no denying that look, it was the look of knowing that Ronnie had always had as a child. How familiar it felt.

Ronnie called out from the back door, 'Mum, it's the phone, shall I answer it?'

'Yes do,' said Minerva, taking Morrigan's tiny hand, 'We're coming now.'

* * *

Minerva swallowed the amber liquid, savouring the warmth as it fired into her belly. 'Say that again Aunt Crow, it's a bad line.'

She cocked her head to the handset and screwed up her eyes as the voice crackled over the airwaves.

'It's never a good reception here, but that's why I like it,' croaked the distant voice, 'keeps people away you know, not many want to visit you in the sticks, and that suits me just fine.'

'You always did like your own company if I remember. Is Roger still going?'

'Stick it up your arse! Stick it up your arse!'

Minerva chuckled into her glass.

'Quieten down, Roger,' crackled Aunt Crow. 'Fifty one years old and that bird is still as rude as ever. I shall miss him though, but he's very easy to look after.'

'Why, where are you going?'

'On a cruise. I want to see the land of the Vikings before I leave for the Summerlands. You don't mind do you?'

'Mind? Why should I mind?'

Minerva felt a twinge of unease as she poured herself another drink.

'I thought you could come and house sit while I'm away. I don't trust no other bugger with my lot. Family is always best don't you think? And you're all I've got left now that your poor mother's gone. Poor Cybele, such a sad life…'

Minerva cleared her throat with another gulp of brandy, 'Oh I see,' she said, not really seeing at all, 'What 'lot' are you talking about Aunt Crow? Do you mean there's more than Roger? And when were you thinking of going on this cruise?'

How nice to be able to do such a thing, she thought, stroking the side of her glass.

'Next week, but don't worry I'll be back for Samhain. Can't miss the new year can I?'

'No, I suppose not.'

She knew how much the Witch's New Year meant to her aunt. A rather dismal childhood spent looking after her mother and that Black Dog of hers was salvaged by the fond memories of Aunt Crow's Treehouse at the bottom of her garden. It was where she'd taken her apprenticeship in the magical arts and she counted herself lucky enough to have learned from someone like Aunt Crow. Their relationship had thrived in those fraught teenage years and it was something she'd never forgotten. Not every Witch had the opportunity to learn the magical ropes in such good company.

With the exception of Roger, of course.

Parrots were not the quietest of creatures but nevertheless, for all his noise and interfering, a bird with Tourette's didn't stop Minerva from learning as much as she could from Aunt Crow.

'So, will you do it, Minerva?' crackled Aunt Crow over the airwaves.

'Yes, of course I'll do it, Aunt Crow, and I'll bring a friend too if you don't mind?'

Isis would be only too glad to accompany her, she was sure of it. Some time away from the magnetic charms of Gerald would do her good.

'No, that's fine with me, although Brenda is very good company you know and requires very little looking after.'

Minerva frowned, 'Is Brenda the housekeeper?

Laughter crackled from the handset. 'In a funny sort of way I suppose she is…'

The silence went on a bit too long for Minerva's liking. 'Aunt

Crow, who is Brenda?'

'My pot-bellied pig of course. You know how I always wanted one, and since I moved out here it's been the perfect environment to have what I set my heart on in the Treehouse all those years ago, not to mention the results of some very concentrated spell work. Like I've always told you Minerva, magic pays off in the most wonderful ways.'

'I've never looked after a pot-bellied pig before,' said Minerva, stroking the rim of her glass. 'Does that mean mucking it out every day?'

She'd done her fair share of stable duties when Ronnie was growing up.

'Just a sweep through and a pick up is all you need to do, she's very clean, you know. And the front room is her favourite place…she likes to share the hearth rug with Didge. They're so good together, I couldn't be more pleased. It was the most unlikely of partnerships at first, but now we all live quite happily together I'm glad to say.'

'Aunt,' said Minerva, slowly, 'are you telling me the pig lives in the house? And who is Didge? Your dog or cat no doubt.'

She couldn't think of any other animals more likely to share a hearth rug.

'Didge is the most wonderful specimen and such a beautiful example of the native species…'

Minerva could feel the beads of sweat forming in her cleavage. 'Native to what?'

'Australia of course. I bought him back from the bush some years ago now. I got quite attached to him – as one does when something takes a shine to you - I could tell by the way he coiled himself around me at night. So comforting! A little unnerving at first but in time I've found it's nothing to worry about…snakes are the friendliest of creatures once you get to know them!'

'I had one as a child if you remember, a yellow snake called Baldrick.'

'Was he small?' said Aunt Crow, before adding quickly, 'Didge will grow on you, I guarantee it. Before you know it, you'll be the closest of pals! Must be something to do with the country. Australians are a particularly friendly bunch I've always found.'

'How big is it?'

'Oh, now you're asking. Last time I measured him he was a good five feet *and* growing. Browns' usually get to about six feet as an adult. But Didge is very sociable, and for anyone with the slightest of nerves about snakes, he's the perfect gentleman…wouldn't hurt a fly!'

'Does he have a cage?' said Minerva with a sinking feeling.

'Oh no, he grew out of that a while ago now…but honestly, you won't know he's there - he literally slips into the background and turns up every now and then.'

'Sounds like a smooth operator,' said Minerva, forcing a smile.

Aunt Crow's laughter crackled loudly from the handset, 'You always did have a way with words Minerva! So you'll come? I'm so looking forward to this trip away…my first in twenty years, you know!'

'Erm, yes Aunt, of course. What does the snake, Didge, eat?'

Her father had always seen to Baldrick's mealtimes.

'Don't worry, they'll be in the freezer. All you have to do is get them out the night before.'

'They?' said Minerva, feeling a chill creeping up her spine.

'The mice come pre-packed you know. Couldn't be easier.'

'Easy bloody peasy! Easy bloody peasy!'

'Roger, quiet!'

'Well, I'm all for an easy life, Aunt,' laughed Minerva, downing the remains of her glass, 'Which reminds me, I need some of your magic please. Since mother went, I've had a rather *unwelcome visitor* making its presence felt and I don't like it...'

'Not the Black Dog?'

'Yes, the very one.'

'Sounds like he could be lost...just needs a bit of guidance in crossing over that's all. He's obviously hanging around you because he doesn't know where your mother's gone.'

'I thought he was already between worlds? How can he need help crossing over?'

'Yes you're right in a way, but it's a complex system, the spirit world – a bit like a motorway with many lanes – one can easily get stuck and lose their bearings.'

'Well, I'd much appreciate it if you could do something about it and move him on and away from me. He's making my life a misery at the moment, and I am *not* my mother. I don't enjoy his company like she did, at all.'

'I'll sort it,' said Aunt Crow, 'Just make sure you do everything to keep yourself as happy as possible in the meantime. He won't stick around if there's laughter and positive energy about, and that'll be easy while you're here won't it?'

'Will it?'

'Oh yes, I can't think of a more uplifting environment than here at Spellstead. It's alive with magic, this place! But, don't you worry Minerva dear, I shall cook up something for the Black Dog. Try one of my herbal baths again, you remember the sort, he'll be on his way in no time. See you soon!'

'Er yes, okay Aunt, and thanks,' said Minerva, staring at the silent handset, 'See you next week.'

She looked up to find Ronnie watching her intently. 'Well, that's my mid- winter break sorted out, a nice cosy bit of house sitting for Aunt Crow.'

'With a pot-bellied pig and a snake for company? Can't think of anything you'd like better.'

'Oh please!' said Minerva, screwing her face up in disgust, 'Isis had better come with me, it's not something I can face alone, that's for certain.'

Ronnie chuckled to herself and with Morrigan balanced on one hip and the crow in a box, she made her way to the front door, calling behind her, 'Look at it as an adventure Mum, you'll be fine!'

'Thank you for the vote of confidence,' said Minerva without looking up. As far as she was concerned, pot-bellied pigs and snakes were not the obvious choices for an adventure. But life was like that sometimes, and choosing wasn't always an option. You just had to make the best of things. And with Isis in the mix, there was no telling what might happen.

If she wasn't mistaken, there was a distinct smell of chaos in the air.

8

Crow Bird

The boat was not the best place for rescued animals, especially a bird. And with dogs like Spaniels and puppies spilling out in all directions, the injured crow was not destined to last long.

Fortunately, there was an alternative and Morrigan clapped her hands in delight every time Ronnie asked her: 'Shall we go to the stables?'

The toddler then proceeded to spend the short journey from the boat to the stable yard squirming about in her car seat and calling out excitedly, 'Crow Bird, my Crow Bird!'

Ronnie was relieved but not surprised when Lazarus took an interest in the pet carrier nesting in the corner of his stable. The two patients soon became acquainted with one another, encouraged by the helping hands of a small person determined in her efforts to introduce them as friends right from the start.

'My pony like Crow Bird,' she told them both firmly as an inquisitive Lazarus peered into the box in his stable. With ears pricked forward he blew gently through the bars with great interest as Ronnie mucked out around them. She thought the squawking was more in acknowledgement than protest and carried on while Morrigan sat on her hunkers watching over both animals. Satisfied there was nothing to fear, she continued to chatter to them both, 'Pony and Crow Bird make friends, *my* friends!'

The squawking was joined by various snorting and the toddler contributing with an odd combination of the two. Ronnie laughed at all three of them. 'You're all bonkers! I've never seen or heard anything like it.'

But it was a happy sound. It was the sound of her daughter enjoying the magic of nature and friendship, reminding her of the rescued pets from her own childhood.

There'd been all sorts of animals - once her mother found an injured bat in the shed outside and and every time the bats swooped around the boat at dusk, she was reminded of those happy days.

Nursing life back to health seemed a completely natural thing for Ronnie to do. She loved to see the life force energy becoming vital again. And with Lazarus especially, as each day passed, the pony grew stronger. Not only did he enjoy the company but he was thriving on it and each day there was an improvement – his eyes soon lost their dullness and his coat's dryness was slowly replaced with the hint of a shine. He reminded her of a butterfly slowly emerging from its cocoon.

'Just don't fly off like they do will you?' She told him one day as he munched happily from his hay net in the corner.

'Like who do?'

Ronnie swung round to see Sophia grinning over the door at her. 'I didn't see you there..!' she laughed. 'Butterflies....once they're fully formed and bursting with colour and life, they take off don't they? I don't want this little fella doing that.'

'And what makes you think he will, Ron? He's thriving on all the attention and care you're giving him – look at him – he's a different animal now and animals aren't daft. They soon learn who they can trust, in fact I think rescue animals are far more loyal to their owners because they're so vulnerable in the first place.'

'I hope you're right when it comes to Lazarus,' said Ronnie patting his bony rump. 'He's pretty special, that's for sure.'

'He'll be fine, Ron. Stop worrying about what hasn't happened!'

'I know it's daft, but after Bob, I guess I don't want that bubble bursting again.'

'Yeah, I can understand that, but how about thinking about what you *do* want instead of what you don't?'

Ronnie laughed. 'You sound just like my mother!'

'And what's that telling you? Great minds and wise women think alike, right?'

'You must be a Witch I reckon,' chuckled Ronnie, turning to the pony, 'I'm surrounded by them, Lazarus!'

'Is that such a bad thing? It's what Diana keeps telling me funnily enough…which reminds me Ron, when can we come round and pick up the puppy? It's her birthday soon.'

'Yes of course, anytime from next week they're good to go. In fact they're literally bursting out of the boat at the moment. We've done all the worming, they just need their injections.'

'Di could come round and do that for you, she's a vet, remember.'

'Come to think of it, that would be a great help Sophia. I was beginning to wonder how the trip to the vets' was going to happen. But if Diana came to the boat and did it - that'd be brilliant. Just let me know when.'

'Will do!' called Sophia, walking away. 'And don't worry about things, eh?'

'No, I won't, and thanks, Sophia, it's good to be back. I've missed our chats.'

'Ditto!'

Sophia's words rang across the yard and Ronnie smiled to herself. Her friend was right, she needed to start trusting in life again. It wasn't as if it was difficult - the evidence was right there in front of her. The crow squawked at Lazarus, hopping from the straw onto his back, and side stepping along the furry platform, let out a raucous cry of triumph: *If I can do it, you can!*

She smiled at him.

'Crow Bird can do it, he can do it..!' Morrigan clapped her hands and jumped a small circle around her mother, whooping with joy. Ronnie grabbed her tiny hands and together they danced round the stable, completely ignored by the munching pony and encouraged by the cackling bird.

Mum always says there's magic in the smallest of things, thought Ronnie, as the glimpse of a shadow swept across the stable. Maybe, this was it.

* * *

Minerva flopped down onto the hard chair and looked up at Isis through sticky strands of red hair. 'So will you come Isis? It's been ages since we went away together on our own. I think it's about time, don't you?'

Isis was smoothing out the folds of silky fabric clinging to her sweaty skin. 'Your Aunt Crow's did you say? Where exactly is that and for how long?'

'Spellstead is about as far away from any kind of normality as you can imagine,' said Minerva, looking around the inside of the village hall at the belly dancing crowd. 'It's somewhere in the highlands of Scotland if I remember correctly. Aunt Crow did it deliberately - she wanted to live in as remote a place as possible - somewhere totally different to the Treehouse and with a bit more room. She needs it of course, for all the animals.'

'Oh, are there many of them?'

The silence that followed was filled with the rustle of Minerva's skirt as she fiddled with the frills, 'I think she has a few in residence, including Roger of course, who's been with Aunt for as long as I can remember. Anyway, I'm sure we can deal with the variety, Isis. It is, after all, the spice of life.'

Isis wasn't sure she liked that word. Variety suggested unorderly and chaotic, which made her nervous, although since meeting Minerva she *had* been willing to try new things. It was the reason she'd changed her whole wardrobe and found herself at a weekly belly dancing class with Kali Patel from the corner shop. If someone as meek as Kali could change into the leader of a vigorous dancing group, then she could become one of those brave dancers too.

'I shall have to have a word with Gerald and see what he's doing first,' said Isis, avoiding Minerva's burning gaze, 'just to be on the safe side. He might have something planned over the next few weeks, you never know.'

'*He* might have something planned? And what about *your* plans? Don't they come first? Honestly Isis, what happened to you? You were doing so well in your post-Derek awakening and stepping into your power at last. You'd *found it* for Goddess sake! Now what? You're going to hand it over to someone else who will take it from you bit by bit and before you know it, you will be a shadow of your stronger and former self, reduced and diluted to nothing more than the weak and whimpering woman you once were. All gone! All gone because you have forgotten who you are!'

A sea of women's faces turned to Minerva and Isis as silence fell upon the room. Isis could feel the heat rising in her cheeks and the sweat pricking the arches of her bare feet.

'There's no need to be so dramatic Minerva, I only said I would ask Gerald what he was doing,' she whispered, her jaw set on the same side as her hairpiece. 'And I haven't forgotten who I am, thanks to your guidance which steered me away from such *weaknesses* and into the arms of the one who loves me. For the first time in my life I have a man putting me first and all I'm doing is respecting Gerald and doing the same. Is that such a bad thing?'

Minerva fiddled with the folds of her skirt and let out a heavy sigh, 'No it isn't, Isis. It isn't at all. But if you could find it in yourself to come to Aunt Crow's with me, I'd very much appreciate it. I could do with some help with her menagerie of *familiars*. And to be honest this Black Dog is still creeping around which I am not entirely happy about - the beast is relentless - not until Aunt Crow's magic has done its job, anyway. I need to get a few of her herbal baths under my belt first and then we'll see if the damn thing is still hanging around.'

'It's still about then?'

'Lurking in the shadows, like all cowards. Why would it do anything else?'

Isis didn't know the answer to that. Her pondering was interrupted by the undulating chimes of an Indian fanfare striking up from the corner where Kali swished and swayed, her hips and belly moving in all kinds of opposite directions. 'To the floor, ladies!' she cried, her words echoing around the hall.

Isis jumped to attention and gently steered Minerva in the direction of the swaying Kali. Who'd have thought sorting newspapers out at dawn and twirling around on a dance floor could be done by the same person? Kali was nothing but an inspiration to the likes of Isis who was discovering more heights of bodily passion than she'd ever conceived possible.

The deep throb of the music pulsated through the half sleeping bodies, teasing them to life until arms and hands took on a life of their own, swirling this way and that, moving together like a living organism joined at the hips and hands by the music. Trance-like and under the spell of Kali and her rubber body, they rippled in a wave of rainbow silks and satins, swishing and flowing as one.

'Let the body remember!' boomed Kali, weaving her way through the sweating bodies.

There's nothing quite like it, thought Isis, her eyes half closed and purring like Bast, her favourite Egyptian Goddess.

Move with your passions and go with the flow!

Gerald's words rang through her mind and she smiled.

Maybe a holiday in the highlands was not such a bad idea after all.

9

Bibles and Banishing

Minerva sank deeper into the mountain of bubbles and breathed in the scent of the herbs. She loved a magical bath. The exorcism powder had been a bit tricky to make, but with a few tweaks here and there, she was pleased with the final result. Cutting up the dried basil, rosemary, rue and yarrow had been easy enough, but adding the graveyard dust to the mix and then into the arrowroot was a messy business. Powders weren't really ideal for baths, but olive oil was an ingredient she didn't have and in this case, herbal sprinkles were better than an oily slick.

Next to the candle and between the taps was a bicycle bell resting on page 109 of her book of shadows…where *BANISHING THE BEAST* stared back at her in large red capitals. She was taking no chances.

Bell, book and candle were top priority and she couldn't afford to leave a hag stone un-turned as far as the Black Dog was concerned. She picked up her mother's old hand mirror with one hand, lit the candle and picked up the book with the other, scanning the page for the first instruction.

'Ah, there you are,' she said to the oak leaf as it fell onto the bubbles and bobbed around, 'I could do with some of your strength. Now where was I? Here it is... *Ring the bell (preferably iron) to repel the negative entity while reciting your sacred text and lighting the beeswax candle to repel all evil.* Hmm,' she mused, glancing around for inspiration as the pages blotted and the ink began to run. Leafing through a book with soggy fingers was not a good idea.

'A hex on you damn dog!' she spat, urgently flicking the lever on the bell. 'I am not putting up with your behaviour one minute longer, do you hear?'

With no readable text to follow, she would have to improvise.

'It looks like a wing and a prayer is in order,' said Minerva to her knee caps, poking like twin peaks through the bubbles. Wiping off a sprig of stray rosemary she pondered for a moment, concentrating hard on the subject at hand. She sensed a sinister presence circling the bath and was glad she'd taken the time to cast the circle before getting in. There was no way it would get through the silver barbed wire she'd wrapped around her aura.

Lifting the hand mirror above the water, she cried out at the dark form staring back at her, 'Be gone you beast of the devil!'

The temperature in the small room dropped to an icy coldness accompanied by the sound of dripping. 'Oh my Goddess!' cried Minerva as a thick, bloody slime oozed from the taps onto the bubbles. It was horrific and if she didn't do something sacred soon it would be too late. She scanned her naked flesh for traces of any gaping wounds. 'You're a clever bastard of a black mongrel if ever I saw one,' she said slowly and deliberately to the dripping taps, 'but not for much longer. This is where it ENDS!'

At first, she didn't hear the knocking.

Drowning out the relentless thudding, the words of a hex flooded into her mind. 'Hear me, you bastard dog!' cried Minerva at the top of her voice.

'Hear me as I cast you out,
To winds of darkness all about
Whip you up and whirl you round
Take you from this sacred ground
To another world from this
Never seen and never missed!
By the power of the moon and sun
I cast you out and IT IS DONE!'

How the magic works is not easy to define but those words fell from her lips like the blood still pouring from the taps. She waited in silence, until the knocking started up again. It was coming from *outside* the bathroom.

'Minerva! Are you okay?'

She knew that voice.

'David, is that really you?'

Minerva clasped both knees and shivered…the water was freezing.

'Of course it's me, I'm coming in.'

The door shook as David pushed against it.

'Oh it's locked!' screamed Minerva, 'I had to try and keep him out…but it hasn't worked!'

The door continued to shake and rattle, 'Keep who out?'

'That *thing*! You know who I mean!'

She couldn't even bring herself to say it for fear of tempting it back through the ether.

The door gave a final jolt and David burst into the room, loose strands from his pony tail sticking to his dog collar. His eyes gleamed with an odd brightness and his cheeks were flushed, 'Good God Minerva, what's happened?!'

'Do you have a bible on you by any chance?' she said, staring into the cold, bloody water.

David fumbled in his waistcoat pocket and pulled out a small brown book, 'I'm never without one, you know that!'

Minerva didn't know anything anymore. Only that now was the time to drive a stake through the heart of this beast and banish it forever.

'You are the hand of God personified!' she cried, hugging her knees closer to her cold body.

David grabbed the towel on the floor and held it up with both hands, 'Minerva get out, you're freezing and no wonder…it's like a fridge in here!'

'Yes it is, but I can't move David, I'm in the icy grip of a force darker than anything I've ever known. It's paralyzing me!'

'Of course you can move, Minerva. Get out! It's all in the —'

'—mind? Don't even say it David. What the hell is all this *stuff* in the water? Correct me if I'm wrong but it's a pretty good example of something not quite right wouldn't you say? It's not every day that blood drips from the taps while taking a bath is it?'

David ran his hand through his hair, 'Yes, but it's not as if you were taking a leisurely bath is it? You had other *intentions*, a particular plan of action…am I right?'

'Yes, of course you're right,' snapped Minerva, 'I'd reached the end of my tether with the bloody thing, you have no idea the effect something like that has on one's life. I saw it all too often with my mother and by the Goddess, I'll be damned if it's going to happen to me too.'

She shot him a look of horror as if the words had already done what she said they would.

'We need to act quickly,' said David, leafing through the small book. He tugged at the crucifix around his neck and unclasped it.

Minerva watched him closely and wondered how he managed to look so attractive in the most unattractive of situations. It was a mystery she pondered on for a few seconds before springing up to full height and leaping awkwardly out of the bath.

'You're a God send...' she sighed, collapsing against his firm torso, 'literally.'

'Do you have any frankincense oil?' said David, studying his bible.

Minerva reached behind them to the cabinet on the wall and handed him a small bottle. He dabbed some of the oil onto his fingers and onto Minerva's forehead. And with the bible in one hand and the crucifix in the other he began to speak in a quiet but firm tone, slowly reciting the words of Psalm 145:

'The Lord is righteous in all he does, merciful in all his acts,
He is near to those who call him, who call to him with sincerity,
He supplies the needs of those who honour him,
He hears their cries and saves them,
He protects everyone who loves him,
But he will destroy the wicked!
I will always praise the Lord,
Let all his holy creatures praise his holy name for ever!'

Minerva listened in silence. She knew the combination of

the oil and the sacred words were the sword and shield they needed against the Black Dog. And as David neared the end of the Psalm she began to feel some life coming back into her frozen body.

David repeated the words again and if Minerva had shut her eyes she would never have known it was him. He now spoke in a dark and menacing tone quite unlike the kind and generous man she thought she knew.

He stood firm like a rock and thrust the crucifix out in front of him at arm's length, *'I command you demon to retreat and return to the fires of hell, where you belong!'*

His eyes grew bigger and his whole body seemed to fill the room with the presence of something she wasn't used to. If this was God, he was certainly a mighty and fearful one. She pulled the towel tighter around her and cowered against the edge of the bath as David repeated the holy words over and over, each time with more authority and power.

She could feel the temperature warming up and noticed a wall of steam rising from the bloody bath. 'David, the water…' she murmured under her breath.

He wasn't listening, continuing instead to cast out the unwanted entity with such a fearsome and concentrated force he didn't look or sound human. He was like a giant cobra spitting out deadly poison and she was caught in the vortex of pure venom as it spun around them, making her feel dizzy and faint.

On and on David went and each time he repeated the Psalm she noticed small beads of sweat glistening on his forehead and upper lip. The walls were shrinking, crowding in around them until the air in her lungs had squashed to the size of a tennis ball and she gasped for more. The feeling in her stomach was intensifying by the minute and unable to control the forces of her body, she belched loudly and fell against David in his trance.

'David, I don't feel at all well,' mumbled Minerva, and reaching out to steady herself, knocked the bible out of his hands. Startled out of his trance, David stepped back as she lost her balance, and together, Minerva and the good book fell into the toilet.

'Minerva, what in heaven's name...!' cried David.
It was not the grand finale she might have hoped for but as the bile rose in her throat she was helpless to stop it and spewed violently onto the bobbing bible in the toilet basin.

'Don't touch me!' cried Minerva, in between the retching. Luckily she was in the perfect position and place for throwing up but the bible had not been so lucky, and all David could do was watch in horror.

'My hair,' mumbled Minerva, hugging the toilet bowl.

'My bible!' cried David, scooping up the thick, red pile of hair and pulling it back sharply.

Minerva felt her body jolting in all directions. Her stomach heaved out the remaining contents as she hung onto the toilet bowl and David hung onto her hair. After minutes which seemed like hours, Minerva opened her eyes, but there was so much hair sticking to her face, it was hard to see anything. She rose slowly from the depths of the toilet bowl, a red beard of hair stuck to her wet cheeks as David hung onto her ponytail with both hands.

'Are you all right?'

'Do I look it?' she groaned underneath him.

David pulled up the naked Minerva. She hung like a rag doll reminding him of an old schoolboy's circus annual of his as

the bearded lady stared back at him, open mouthed. It was not the kind of sight he was used to seeing, just as an exorcism was not the usual kind of vicarly duty he was used to performing. 'Minerva, let's get you covered up.'
He grabbed the bath towel and wrapped it loosely around her shuddering body. 'You're cold.'

'I don't know what I am,' wailed Minerva, wiping her hairy mouth with a corner of the towel, 'Has it gone?'

David glanced around the steamy room, 'I think our mission is accomplished, yes.'

'And the bible?'

'Yes.' David winced at the sight of the bobbing bible below, 'Drowned together I'm afraid.'

'The good and the bad, you mean?'

'Now you've put it like that, yes.'

'Maybe it was meant to happen like that.'

'What do you mean?' asked David, patting the mass of red hair down behind her head.

'Wasn't it an act of God?'

'You mean the bible and the beast?'

'Yes, they were the perfect contrast weren't they? And now they're both down the pan. It won't come back will it, David? Tell me it won't!'

She buried her head into his chest and coughed as she breathed in the lingering scent of frankincense.

'I'm telling you it won't come back Minerva, trust me...it's gone.'

He said the words with such finality she was tempted to believe him. 'I *want* to believe you David, honestly I do, but I shall attend to a few cautionary things first, just to set my mind at rest.'

David sighed and squeezed her gently, 'I take it that you are referring to some magical housekeeping? Only to be expected by someone of your position I suppose.'

Minerva pulled away sharply and reached for her bicycle bell and a large pot of salt on the window sill.

She began to ring the bell loudly while sprinkling the salt in thick layers all around them. 'I shall be needing some fenugreek seeds if my memory serves me right.'

David wondered how she could remember anything after what had just happened. 'And what do you need them for?' he said, checking his crucifix for foreign bodies and slipping it back under his dog collar.

'Protection of course, you wash your hair three times in the tincture,' said Minerva, scraping the sticky red mass into a bun.

David felt a slight shudder as he turned off the light and opened the bathroom door. 'Of course, it goes without saying, doesn't it?' he said, glancing sideways behind them. 'Shall we go and have a look for some, and something to revive the senses while we're at it?'

'What a splendid idea, vicar,' said Minerva, loosening the towel away from her shoulders, 'Perfect for post-demonic fatigue.'

She led the way down the stairs, pouring the salt and ringing the bell, before entering the warmth of the kitchen.

'It's not every day I get to encounter such dark territories,' said David. 'After all, there's no substitute for experience in these things. It doesn't do any harm to build the required muscles for when the enemy strikes does it?'

Minerva squinted as his crucifix caught the light. 'No it doesn't, in fact it helps to keep in mind that the enemy…' she paused, unscrewing the lid of the brandy bottle, '…is always closer than you think.'

10

Puppy Love

Ronnie watched Joe throw his baseball cap on and grab a bunch of keys before turning to wave at her. 'Another day, another dollar,' he sang, springing across the deck to kiss her, 'Good luck with those pups today, how many we got walking the plank?'

'One's going this morning and another two in the afternoon,' said Ronnie, checking her phone, 'And not before time either, they're all over the place.'

'You don't have to tell me that,' he laughed, 'Mad bunch of Houdinis' they are! Good job I managed to build the run for them eh? Nice bit of luck finding that wood I reckon…'

'I'm not sure how much longer my nerves can take it,' said Ronnie, 'I'm the one who has to deal with them climbing in and out of every nook and cranny. This place is hardly the right environment for them is it?'

'It wouldn't matter where they were, they'd still outgrow their space – it's what happens with young animals. Anyway, it's only the last few weeks which have been a bit mad, not like it's been the whole time is it?'

'No, but I've got Morrigan to sort out as well as Lazarus…and now crow Bird as well.'

'Yeah, well you will keep picking up these waifs and strays,' he winked and kissed her cheek, 'The girl with a heart of gold.'

She pulled away from him, 'This heart of gold can't take much more, Joe. It's all right for you, leaving me to deal with it all every day!'

'Hang on a minute Ron, I do have a job to do you know. It's not as if I'm bumming off for no reason *and* I do look after all of you into the bargain!'

She looked down at the coffee mug and sighed, 'I know, I know and I'm sorry…it's just that sometimes it all feels a bit much. I'm just tired, that's all.'

'We can all say that. Anyway I've got a job to do, must be off.'

She shot him a pleading look, 'Look, I'm sorry, just ignore me!'

'No I can't do that I'm afraid, you're too gorgeous for a start…but I must go.'

He squeezed her shoulders together and looked deep into her eyes, 'Just stop worrying Ron, eh? Everything has a way of working out, the pups are moving on now, they'll be off out of our hair. Next thing you know you'll be saying you miss them!'

She tried to stop laughing, 'How did you guess?'

'Because you're not the only one who's psychic that's why!'

He pecked her on the lips and shot out of the boat with one hand raised to the sky, 'And I predict that I won't have a job if I hang around for too much longer. You're too much of a distraction Rhiannon, you know that?' He turned and winked at her, 'But I wouldn't have it any other way! Oh and did I tell you, I'm out tonight rehearsing with the lads. Meet us down the Druid for a drink after?'

He was getting further away from her. 'If I can chat Mum up to have Morrigan, then yes I will...' she called after him softly, 'Love you Cap'n!'

'Thank the Goddess for that!' He turned and saluted the brightly painted Freya above the door.

Ronnie felt an affinity with the Viking female deity, quite different to her mother's leanings which tended to be more Celtic in origin. She wondered if it really mattered what culture or pantheon one was drawn to and the more she pondered over it, the more she thought that it was actually the other way round. It was what her mother had often said to her when she was a child...you didn't choose the Gods.

They chose you.

It was how the web worked...how the magical threads were spun and weaved, through cultures and centuries and lifetimes. The Witch's perspective transcended all those things because in the end they were unimportant.

Ronnie was beginning to understand. She was beginning to see that the Gods and Goddesses were archetypes all with their own characters and patterns of behaviour. They were aspects of divinity personified through all kinds of belief systems. She must talk to her mother about it, she knew far more about these things than Ronnie did. But the thing was, her mother had told her that the mysteries remained hidden, revealing themselves only to those who were ready for the knowledge and had earned the responsibility of that power.

Knowledge is power, Rhiannon!

Ronnie tried to stop the thoughts running around her head, they were beginning to feel like they were not her own, but more like an age old wisdom reaching out to her through the ether.

'Nothing like the truth is there?'

Ronnie spun round and saw the bright colours of Freya glowing from the side of the boat. She could have sworn she'd heard a voice.

'Yes you did, it was mine.'

She breathed in quickly as she searched for the sound of the voice outside of her own head. 'Who are you? Where are you?' said Ronnie warily, scanning her surroundings for evidence of someone. *Anyone.*

Eventually, her gaze returned to Freya and her cloak of feathers, her chariot and her cats. The voice continued, 'I am the mystery and the unfolding, the voice and the guiding hand of that which you seek but do not know yet.'

Ronnie frowned at the Goddess, 'I don't understand what you're saying, at all. It all sounds a bit cryptic to me, not unlike a conversation with my own mother, actually.'

The sound of soft laughter rippled across the deck of the boat, fading into the distance. 'That is because I *am* the mother in a way.'

Ronnie wasn't laughing. 'What is it you want? Because I've got a heavy schedule today.'

'Indeed,' rumbled the voice, 'Exactly my point. Take the runes from the third cabin room – they are hidden behind an old beam - and learn to use them. Play with them at first, as you would if you were getting to know anything or anyone. When we play, we learn…'

Ronnie couldn't think why she would need any more on her plate than she already had. She knew how long it had taken her mother to learn and master the tarot – these divination systems were complex and required concentration and commitment to get to grips with them. But she was intrigued to know more about them and what they could do. 'Did they belong to Ropey?' she asked, noticing how Freya's cloak of feathers shimmered with every colour of the rainbow.

'Passed down by ancestors, yes. But he never used them, preferring instead to only admire them occasionally, when he remembered. However, when the spiritual warrior is ready, the battlefield appears and the weapons show themselves. The runes are both sword and shield. They are magical tools for the warrior if he is brave enough to learn how to use them.'

Ronnie was gone before the Goddess had finished speaking, hurrying down the tiny corridors of the boat. The third cabin was the spare room and full of bags and boxes and she fought her way through to the beam across the back where at first she found nothing, only dust and dead spiders between the wood and the wall. Feeling foolish to have listened to a disembodied voice of all things, she was ready to give up.

That's when she saw the green, cloth bag stuffed far back into the corner of the wall and she pulled it out slowly, feeling the tingle in her hands as she did. Pulling the cord free she opened the neck of the soft, hessian pouch and looked inside. It was full of stones. And without studying them further she made her way back to Freya, clutching the bag.

'Now you have a tool from the water; be like the otter and play!' said the Goddess, her voice fading as the colours dulled against the wood.

Ronnie opened her mouth to speak, but stopped. Freya had gone. Reaching deep into the bag she enjoyed the feel of the cold, smooth pebbles, every one different in size and shape. She picked one out and held it up to eye level, turning it around between her thumb and forefinger, noticing the symbol painted in black on the pale sandstone. It looked similar to the letter F.

Rolling the smooth stone around between her fingers she wondered where it had come from. She'd seen many of these sand stones on the beach. What ancestors had made these?

Her thoughts were interrupted by a familiar voice calling her name in the distance. It wasn't Freya this time, but a waving and smiling Sophia, bouncing across the yard to the pontoons.

'Ron, there you are…you all right?'

'Yes, why don't I look it?'

'You've got that faraway look about you, like you're somewhere else. You haven't been at Joe's stash have you?!'

Ronnie frowned and then chuckled at Sophia's concerned expression, 'You know I don't touch the stuff Soph, not something that's ever appealed to me.'

'No, you don't need it Ron, you're completely fine in your own place of other-worldliness. I've always envied you for that.'

'Have you?' That surprises me, you being the epitome of logic and reason.'

'Working in law isn't all it's cracked up to be, you know. There's a lot of stress with the job, which is fine most of the time…'

'But you need your time off right? Which is why you spend so much time down the yard with that wonder horse of yours!'

'And why I'm here to pick up a puppy for that girlfriend of mine.'

Ronnie clapped her hands together, 'Of course, I *knew* there was a perfectly good reason why you were here. Come this way madam.'

The two friends fell into step beside each other and made

their way to the large pen on the grassy patch beside Freya's Return.

'Joe's made a good job of this hasn't he?' shouted Sophia, struggling to make herself heard above the sound of excited barking.

'He definitely has, and it's all with recycled wood from the boat yard, we didn't pay for a thing! He can pretty much turn his hand to anything practical,' said Ronnie, 'which has been a god send with this little lot, as you can see. We couldn't keep them on the boat the whole time – especially not now!'

Sophia laughed, 'Oh my goodness, they're even more gorgeous than the photos. How the hell am I going to choose one?'

'Quite easily I hope,' said Ronnie, unlatching the gate and ushering Sophia through into a sea of bouncing black, white and tan, 'With a bit of luck, I think you'll find one'll choose you!'

As the pups ran towards them, Sophia squealed with delight, 'Yeah, but not all of them!'

'Well the idea is that you have to choose *one*,' said Ronnie, bending down to greet the lively pack. 'So you've managed to keep it from Diana?'

'Just about,' said Sophia, picking up a floppy eared bundle of black and white fur, 'I think she's onto the scent, though. She found the dog basket I bought and wrapped up only yesterday and started asking questions. It was a tough call but I managed to steer her off course. Told her it was a present for one of my clients!'

Ronnie laughed, 'Oh no, spoiler alert! It's just as well that you'll be taking one home later, then. What a lovely surprise.'

'Yes I know,' said Sophia, trying to avoid having her face

washed by the over-exuberant pup, 'I've got a feeling we're in for some fun times ahead with our new addition...'

'Is that the one then?' said Ronnie, 'He's taken a shine to you!'

Sophia buried her nose into the puppy and came up for air with a huge grin. 'I think you're right Ron. I'm in love! And so will Diana be when she sees him, I can't wait to see her face.'

'Well that was easy,' laughed Ronnie, 'I'll get your puppy pack with his papers in, all present and correct. Di came over and gave them their final jab last week. I feel a bit of a fraud really, but I was a good actress and didn't let it slip.'

'You did a good job Ron, and they're all a credit to you, a stunning litter. And this little fella, he's coming home with me!'

'I'm so glad you're having one Sophia. Not only from the point of view of knowing he's got a great home but it will be lovely to hear about his progress and actually *see* him.'

'Oh of course,' said Sophia, passing the squirming puppy over to Ronnie and grabbing her bag, 'He'll be a regular visitor to the yard no doubt and will get plenty of exposure to other animals. Well socialized they call it, don't they?'

She handed Ronnie an envelope and took the puppy back into her arms.

'I hope that's not the full amount,' said Ronnie awkwardly.

'And why wouldn't it be?' asked Sophia, 'You don't think I'd assume any different do you? And before you say *anything*, please don't and we'll leave it at that.'

Ronnie knew better than to argue with Sophia when she spoke in that tone. It was the voice of the lawyer she usually saved for the courts and the voice of authority which made Sophia so good at her job. Not many challenged it and Ronnie wasn't about to now. 'That's very kind of you, thank you,' she said gracefully, tucking the envelope deep inside the pocket of her jacket, 'Much appreciated.'

'You're very welcome Ron. I know how hard you've both worked to raise this lot, especially with everything else going on at the same time, but you've done it and they're a credit to you, really they are. You deserve every penny.' She touched her friend's arm, 'They cost enough to keep after all, and you need to take your time into account too. It all adds up doesn't it?'

'I suppose it does, it's just that with friends it's different.'

'Not this one,' said Sophia firmly, 'It's an absolute fair exchange, so accept it and continue in the same vein with the rest of the gang, eh? You've earned it.'

'You're a good friend Sophia,' said Ronnie, giving her a hug, 'I'll see you later at the yard.'

Sophia settled the bouncing pup into the cage in her car and stood by the driver's door, 'You've done wonders with that pony, Ron, he's a different animal thanks to you.'

'It's not just me,' said Ronnie, 'there's something about him, he's a strong little thing and Morrigan loves him so I guess they're made for each other, and then there's Crow Bird of course...'

'You never do anything by halves do you?' laughed Sophia, climbing into the driver's seat, 'Make sure you treat yourselves with the puppy funds eh?'

'A few drinks down the Druid later is in order, I reckon,' said Ronnie, scanning the pontoons for signs of Joe, 'We'll be down there if you get a moment tonight, which you probably won't, not with the new arrival.'

'No,' said Sophia starting the engine, 'I've a feeling we'll be otherwise occupied, thank you!'

Ronnie waved as Sophia drove away. She felt for the envelope in her pocket and pulled out the rune stone she'd picked earlier. She looked at it, inspecting the F symbol painted onto its smooth surface and thought of Freya and fertility and fortune.

Some things were too obvious to ignore.

11

Sneaking Suspicion

Minerva was looking forward to getting away.

A couple of weeks at Aunt Crow's place was just what she needed to clear her head and her energy fields. Now the Black Dog had gone, she felt like a new person. Gone were the shadows and dark edges to her days. What a relief it was to be floating on a cloud instead of underneath one.

'What do you reckon, Tilda, is he up to the job?' Minerva called to the bright red monkey boots under Mr. Morris's bonnet one chilly Saturday morning.

'Depends what sort of job you mean Minerva,' came the gruff reply, 'I take it your planning a journey of some sort, am I right?'

As far as Minerva was concerned, the things that were right with Tilda were few and far between. Especially since the handyman turning up on her doorstep in a boiler suit for years, now showed up in purple dungarees, matching French beret and a variation of brightly coloured accessories. Today it was an orange chiffon scarf knotted tightly on one side around his thick neck. Even for the broader minded individual, whom Minerva liked to think she was, it was a lot to digest.

'You would be absolutely right, yes Tilda,' said Minerva, looking for any sign of curtains twitching. 'It's about a hundred and fifty miles to Jockitchshire from here, not a great distance but I would dearly love to make the journey in Mr. Morris, my old faithful. To resort to public transport would be a real disappointment, if you know what I mean.'

Tilda nodded, she knew exactly what Minerva meant. You didn't spend years working for a customer and not get to know them. Call it women's intuition but Tilda did seem to have an uncanny knack of knowing these things.

'That's exactly why I wouldn't have anyone else working for me,' said Minerva, putting down a mug of tea and a plate of garibaldis on the drive. 'With you Tilda, I never have to explain myself. We're on the same page.'

'That's absolutely it, Minerva,' said Tilda coming up for air, her beret slipping back to reveal a receding hairline, 'I always know where I am with you.'

Minerva wasn't sure she could say the same about Tilda, but smiled sweetly and nodded to the plate of garibaldis. Tilda took a handful and popped two into her bristly mouth, followed by the same again.

'So will he make it do you think?' asked Minerva, trying not to stare at Tilda and the rapidly disappearing biscuits.

'I don't see any reason why not,' Tilda glugged down the tea and wiped her mouth with the sleeve of her blouse. 'I shall give him a good going over and that will set you up for your journey. Monday was it?'

'Er yes, that's right,' said Minerva with a fixed smile, 'That's very good to know, Tilda, thank you. I shall notify Isis and we can make our arrangements. Best to set out nice and early I think, before the roads get too busy. Thank you, I feel so much better knowing he's been *done,* if you know what I mean?'

'Oh yes,' said Tilda, tugging sharply at her beret, 'When it comes to getting things done, Minerva, I'm your man.'

***

'Have you told Gerald yet?' barked Minerva down the phone as she watched Tilda's burly figure disappearing down the drive.

There was a long pause before Isis answered, 'I was going to tell him tonight.'

'Tonight? Aren't you leaving it a bit late? Don't you think you could have told him a bit sooner? We're going on Monday!'

'Not really,' said Isis, 'Gerald will be fine. He doesn't get uptight about these kind of things, and he's not the jealous sort as far as I can tell.'

Minerva poured a large shot of brandy into her second cup of tea and popped the last garibaldi into her mouth. 'One never really knows a person's true colours Isis, until the situation presents itself. After all, if you think about it, you haven't known him that long, have you?'

'Long enough to feel as comfortable as I do,' said Isis in a frosty tone.

'Do you have a date for the handfasting yet?'

'The spring seems to be favourite at the moment although we don't have an actual date yet. But it's definitely on the cards, and you'll be the first to know when we do!'

'Good,' said Minerva, 'Now Isis, please prepare for an early get-away on Monday. Aunt Crow is expecting us by mid-afternoon at the latest.'

'Are we going in Mr. Morris?'

'We are indeed. Tilda has just given him the once over and according to her or *him* - whichever takes your fancy - all is well.'

'Is it?'

'Yes of course,' said Minerva, 'Don't worry Isis, I know you're not the best of passengers but I have a spell for jaded nerves, it's all sorted and bubbling away in the cauldron, nothing to worry about, you'll see.'

'Right,' said Isis slowly, trying not to fear the worst. It was a hard habit to break, but sometimes, as Gerald said, these things cropped up as a test to overcome the fear monster. Nothing to fret about at all, thought Isis, placing her trust fully in Minerva and Mr. Morris.

Minerva thought it best not to mention just yet what was waiting for them at Aunt Crow's. Hopefully, with the spell for Isis in full swing on the journey up there, it wouldn't be any cause for concern. However, should any more magic be needed, Aunt Crow had a very comprehensive, magical library and there'd be plenty of opportunity for spells to combat any residual fear and worry. And *perfect* for experimentation purposes.

What more could a Witch ask for?

* * *

Ronnie counted out the notes slowly, neatly folding each one before placing them in an envelope and stamping PUPPY FUND on it in thick felt pen. She thought about Freya and the rune stone and tucked it behind the old teapot. The small fortune would come in very handy: Morrigan needed a few clothes and she'd been wanting to buy Lazarus a rug for the winter, plus a book on Rune stones would be useful. Since her college life had come to an abrupt end with the arrival of Morrigan, she had missed her studies. And now it seemed, instead of her choosing her subjects, they were choosing her.

Joe would finally be able to afford to buy that new guitar he'd been talking about and drooling over for months. And for once, the end of the year need not be the stressful time it always was with the usual financial pressure of Christmas. She breathed a sigh of relief and gave a silent nod of thanks to Freya. She was looking forward to meeting Joe at the Old Druid later, and was sure her mother wouldn't mind having Morrigan for a couple of hours, especially if there was a bottle of brandy thrown in for good measure.

It was time to celebrate. If she went to the stables now to feed and bed down Lazarus, she would make the pub just about the same time Joe did. On her way out she grabbed the green hessian pouch and slipped it into her pocket, feeling the smooth curves of the stones with her fingers and humming to herself.

* * *

A few hours later, Ronnie bounced into the Old Druid's dimly lit bar to join Joe. He stood with his back to her, deep in conversation and huddled over his drink with someone else. As she got nearer she realised it was Allan Key, the new drummer in the band.

'Hey guys,' said Ronnie, squeezing Joe's shoulder and beaming at him when he turned around.

'Well here she is...' said Joe, grinning widely, 'talk of the devil and she will appear!'

'Oh yeah? And what might that be about then?'

Ronnie felt for the runes in her pocket,

'A strange looking devil but a very radiant looking one, if you don't mind me saying,' said Allan, bending down to take her hand and kissing it.

Ronnie smiled awkwardly at the ruddy cheeked Allan, ignoring the uneasiness in the pit of her stomach. 'Can I get you two a drink?'

Turning to Joe she showed him the envelope, 'Three pups gone today!'

'Blimey Ron, that's a bit of good news and couldn't have come at a better time eh? Kind of fits in with our news, doesn't it Allan?'

Ronnie saw the two of them swap looks before Allan gestured to Ernie for drinks all round.

'So come on, tell me...' said Ronnie, looking from one to the other.

Neither would look at her, choosing instead to indulge in their full pints of Druid fluid fresh from the tap.

Joe was the first to break the silence, 'Allan's got us a tour, Ron. It could be our big break, what d'ya think of that?'

'When?'

'Oh it won't be until next year,' said Allan, 'There's a lot of arrangements to make and these things take time to sort out.'

Ronnie stared hard at Joe, 'When?'

'January, maybe?'

'How long for?' said Ronnie, not taking her eyes off him.

'A week. Two weeks at the most,' replied Joe, beginning to look sheepish. 'I've still got a couple of weeks holiday to take before April.'

'What about Christmas?'

Joe frowned at her, 'What *about* Christmas?'

'You always take a week off at Christmas!'

Allan shifted from one foot to the other, taking a large gulp of his drink and looking away.

Joe shot her a pleading look, 'Ron, we're talking two weeks max, at the most. It's not forever! Anyway, you could come as well if you wanted to—'

Ronnie gave an awkward laugh, 'As if I could manage that, Joe!'

Joe shrugged his shoulders and knocked back half of his pint, 'Look, the offer's there if you want it okay? It's not as if you're banned from coming on tour with us but sometimes…'

'Sometimes *what?*'

'Sometimes, you don't make it easy on yourself! For Christ sake, anybody'd think I was heading off to the front line or something. It's an opportunity for the band - *my band* - to get out there and show people what we're made of. Why wouldn't you think that's a good idea? Allan's got a few contacts and it's these sort of connections that you need to push forward if you gonna' get anywhere in this world.'

'Sometimes it's what the music needs,' said Allan almost apologetically, 'to push beyond its comfort zone, it's where stuff can happen.'

Ronnie glared at him. 'What kind of *stuff?*'

She thought of Posh Bird and her father, she thought of being on the boat alone and how old wounds never quite went away for good.

Allan began to drum his fingers against the side of his pint glass. 'Opportunities can happen anywhere Ronnie, but they're more likely to show up when you put yourself out there, right where they are. It's the law of probability in action.'

'You don't have to blind me with science, I'm not stupid!'

Ronnie could feel her cheeks burning as the silky voiced Allan went to say something else but stopped, choosing instead, to finish his drink to the incessant tapping of fingers.

Joe put his hand on her arm but she brushed it off and glared at him. 'Don't patronize me please!'

Joe held his hands up, 'Take it easy, Ron. Wasn't expecting this sort of reaction that's for sure!'

Ronnie could feel the heat pricking the back of her neck. 'Well, there's a little surprise for you then. I don't suppose you were thinking of breaking the news a little more *discreetly* were you? Perhaps when we were on our own maybe?'

Joe narrowed his eyes at the bottom of his glass, tipping it straight back and swallowing hard. But before he could say anything, Allan stood up quickly, fishing in his pockets for a set of keys. 'Joe, I'll be off, mate. Let me know when the next rehearsal is and I'll get those numbers sorted out. I'm almost there with them now. Bloody good songs!'

He shot out long white fingers to Joe's brown, weathered hand and Ronnie felt the niggle in her gut again. Something wasn't right but she didn't know what.

'I'll be in touch Allan,' said Joe, shaking his hand firmly. 'Cheers for coming down. I appreciate your input, mate.'

'Anytime Joe. You know where I am...' called Allan as he walked towards the door, 'Nice to see you Ronnie!'

The door slammed shut, leaving a heavy silence behind it while Ernie began to shuffle bottles around and whistle loudly to himself. Within less than a minute, the opening bars of *You Are My Sunshine* rippled across from the jukebox and Joe looked up at Ronnie with a grin.

'Don't even think about it...' she said, setting her jaw.

'Oh, come on Ron, lighten up,' said Joe, 'It's not all that bad is it?'

'Let's hope not,' she whispered into her drink.

12

Hag Stones and Retrogrades

Monday morning arrived dark and early along with Mercury retrograde.

Stopping at Hag Stone services seemed like a good idea at the time - the call of nature was one thing that couldn't be ignored – but when Mr. Morris refused to start again, Minerva's patience, already worn thin with Isis and her passenger nerves, was running out.

'I should've known the spell might not work as well as usual,' said Minerva, spitting out bits of coffee flavoured cardboard. 'Damn Mercury and it's backward mentality!'

Isis continued to breathe heavily into a brown paper bag while Minerva turned the key in the ignition for the umpteenth time. 'Minerva,' she spluttered in between breaths, 'isn't that the definition of something…when you do the same thing over and over again, expecting different results?'

'What madness are you talking about now, Isis?' snapped Minerva.

Isis wheezed and took a deep breath in, 'We've been sitting in this car park for over half an hour now and you have turned that key over and over to make Mr. Morris start.'

'*And* I've repeated the usual spell to no avail, which is most unusual,' said Minerva, stroking the walnut dashboard.

'That is my point,' gasped Isis before diving back into the paper bag, 'How much longer are you going to carry on for? Shouldn't we be thinking of an alternative plan?'

Minerva stopped and turned to Isis, 'I feel a touch of pot and a black kettle in the air if you don't mind me saying so, *Isis*. You have also been sitting there repeatedly doing the same thing, and can I ask, is it any different now than it was?'

'What do you mean? Can I breathe better?'

'Isn't that why you do it?'

'Well yes, of course it is.'

Minerva stared hard at the gear stick, 'And are you feeling calmer?'

'Yes, I suppose I am,' said Isis.

'So why are *you* still doing the same thing over and over? Don't you see?' said Minerva through gritted teeth.

Isis huffed out a big sigh and stuffed the brown paper bag back into the orange silk handbag beside her.

'I must say,' said Minerva, 'I'd have thought Aunt Crow of all people would know better than to plan this when Mercury is not at its most harmonious!'

'Do you mean retrograde?'

'Yes I do! Can't you feel it working its particularly rude and selfish magic upon us? It's a tiresome planet when it goes into reverse. Nothing ever works out quite how you want it to, travel and communications especially!'

'Oh I see what you mean,' said Isis, feeling a flicker of understanding as her breathing became steadier, 'Do you think we should ring her and let her know?'

'Know what?'

'That we're going to be late!'

'Definitely not,' said Minerva, wiping the steam off the windscreen, 'Time to turn things around Isis...it's what every Witch does best. If mercury can do it, then so can we!'

Minerva leaned across to the glove compartment and pulled out a purple drawstring bag. Delving inside, she took out a large, ugly looking stone with a misshapen hole and held it up to the dim light of a murky sun. Slowly and deliberately, she began to chant:

'Hag of day and hag of night
Imbued with power and sacred light
From above and to the ground, Inside out and turn around
Good for travel, good for health
Be you known and show yourself!'

Isis wondered what kind of magic Minerva was up to now. She wasn't quite sure how reverse retrograding could work, but if spending time with Minerva had taught her anything, it was to consider the idea of possibility in any way, shape or form it showed up in. It was to believe that things *would* get better by using the powers of the earth and shaping them into words and spells.

Magic was in the hands of the magician every time. Nothing was more exciting than that, thought Isis, staring dreamily out of the window.

The slamming of the driver's door made her jump and she watched Minerva marching through the rows of parked cars to a pick-up truck in the far corner of the service station. The two men casually leaning against the truck stopped talking as Minerva approached and Isis watched, intrigued as the men became enthralled with the animated Minerva. With her flaming red hair flowing and arms waving back and forth under her purple poncho she gestured from Mr. Morris to the truck and back again. Like a dancer, she weaved and turned in the most subtle of ways, never losing eye contact and holding their attention completely.

Isis caught sight of the hag stone as Minerva passed it from one hand to the other. But the men weren't watching the stone, they didn't even know it was there. They were watching Minerva, probably not even hearing her or seeing the web she was so intricately weaving between them, around them and through them. Every move she made drew them closer in, every turn of her head kept them captivated as she worked her magic into life. Isis clapped her hands and suppressed a squeal of delight.

She had never seen anything like it.

Ten minutes later Minerva returned to Mr. Morris and dropped the hag stone back into the purple pouch after hugging it close to her heaving chest. She said nothing, but sat there with her eyes closed.

Isis played with the corners of her bag, pulling at the silky threads until it frayed as she wrapped her ankles in knots around each other. 'That was amazing,' she gushed, 'Like watching a human peacock in action!'

'It was the hag stone that did it,' said Minerva. 'There's something about a piece of mother earth that you've found yourself. Works every time.'

'What *did* happen?' asked Isis, 'You had those men in the palm of your hand as well as the hag stone!'

Minerva chuckled, 'Yes, they went under in no time didn't

they? Decent enough blokes, though, decent enough to tow us the rest of the way.'

'Really?'

'According to them they were going that way anyway and *one* of them actually knows Aunt Crow would you believe?'

'No!'

'Yes, Isis. Be assured, this is how magic happens. Hag stone power is the strongest there is.'

She handed the purple pouch to Isis, 'Put that in your bag, we shall be needing it at Aunt Crow's.'

'Will we?' said Isis, plopping it into the silky bag by her feet.

'Indeed,' said Minerva in a serious tone, 'Mercury's influence is everywhere. Always best to be prepared, wherever one goes.'

'Yes, I'm beginning to see that,' said Isis, closing the bag shut, 'Have I got time to spend another penny?'

She looked across at the two men who were busying themselves around the truck with a rope and glancing over at Mr. Morris. Minerva was busy craning her head at the rear view mirror rescuing a straying clump of red hair, 'Don't be long Isis, they said they want to get going fairly soon and we don't want to be holding them up. It won't do to *un-do* the magic now, will it?'

'How long does it last for?' said Isis, scrambling out of the door.

'As long as the hag stone dictates and I've programmed it for another three hours so we should be okay,' said Minerva. 'They said it shouldn't take longer than a couple at the most, as long as there are no hitches of course.'

'Of course,' said Isis, clutching her bag with one hand and nudging her hairpiece over with the other. As she tottered over to the toilets, she pulled out the brown paper bag from

the bottom of her bag and threw it in the nearest bin.
She wouldn't be needing that anymore. Letting go of unnecessary baggage was something she was getting better at, particularly since Minerva and herself had become friends.

It was always a comfort to know you could trust the magic completely.

* * *

Two hours and a family pack of maltesers later, Mr. Morris was quivering along at a steady pace on the pick-up truck. Slowly the landscape began to change from flats and marshlands to rolling hills and valleys. And Minerva and Isis took great delight as the scenery opened up before them in great patches of colour as they entered Jockitchshire.

'I could get used to this, said Minerva, hands behind her head and feet on the dashboard. 'A little *refreshment* wouldn't be a bad idea at all, would it?'

'We've just had some,' said Isis, 'Oh, I see what you mean, yes! I quite forgot you're not driving. A tipple is allowed is it?'

'I can't think why not,' said Minerva, reaching behind her to a box of martelle nestled firmly between their two suitcases. 'The only thing is, I didn't bring any glasses. Do we still have those cardboard things from earlier?'

Isis felt inside the side pockets of the doors and fished out two squashed and soggy paper cups, 'Better than nothing, as you'd say.'

Minerva chuckled, 'Would you believe it, I'm becoming predictable of all things! Although, these days I'm inclined to think that mystery is over- rated. It's almost a thing of the past.'

'Are you saying you're past it?' said Isis, turning the cardboard cups upside down onto a thick wad of toilet paper.

Minerva took out a full bottle of brandy from the box and held it up to the light. 'Not at all,' she said, 'I've never felt more chipper. David says I'm in my prime, he likes a mature woman. What about you Isis, does Gerald appreciate the spirit of maturity when he sees it do you think?'

Isis in her attempt to reshape the soggy cups as best she could was now holding them carefully on her knees. 'I'd like to think he does, yes,' she said, deep in thought, 'He told me I'm very different to the women he's usually attracted to – he wants to look after me – so I'm not sure that's a sign of maturity as such is it?'

With a steady hand, Minerva poured the brandy into both cups and paused before replacing the lid, 'It's a different kind of dynamic you and Gerald have between you and as long as it works and you're both happy, that's all that matters. Gerald's obviously more comfortable as a father figure and as long as you stay as you are and retain your child-like charm, you'll be attractive to him.'

'Will I?'

'Oh yes, the only drawback for you is you will have to remain forever young but I don't think that'll be difficult, Isis. In the meantime, I shall endeavour to concoct an elixir of youth for your consumption only, with the exception of allowing me the odd sip or two when my mature spirit needs reviving, of course.'

'I think I can manage that,' said Isis, raising her soggy cup to Minerva's.

'To the old and the new,' said Minerva, 'And a decent holiday into the bargain. We deserve it.'

The brandy went down a treat, which was just as well because by the time they reached Aunt Crow's the rain was coming down in sheets and the wind was howling around the outbuildings like a banshee.

* * *

Mr Morris came off the pick-up truck quite differently to how he went on. Minerva was still behind the wheel, hands gripping on tightly as they were lowered to the ground. It wasn't exactly a straight forward operation, and the two men, mesmerized by Minerva's charms at the service station, stood with bemused faces as she drove off the ramp at Spellstead Hall.

And even with half a bottle of brandy inside her, Minerva managed to look vibrant and untamed. Her flashing green eyes and scarlet hair made a striking contrast although the same could not be said for her co-ordination. Consequently, Mr. Morris veered off the pick-up truck at an angle.

One of the men leaned in through the half open driver's window to where Minerva sat slumped over the wheel. 'Are you all right in there love?'

'Absolutely,' she beamed at him, 'I can't thank you enough for the ride.'

'Our pleasure,' smirked the truck driver, a thin roll-up dangling between broken teeth. 'Couldn't leave you damsels in distress alone to your own devices now could we?'

He caught a glimpse of the half empty brandy bottle out of the corner of his eye and laughed, 'Looks like you've been having a bit of fun into the bargain, and why not indeed?!'

They seemed decent enough chaps, thought Minerva, even

if neither of them had any clothes sense. In spite of the cold weather, they stood outside Mr. Morris, thick, bare arms protruding from worn out t-shirts with not a hair standing on end.

Minerva turned her head in the direction of a familiar voice carried by the wind, 'You're here at last. I was beginning to get worried about you!'

Aunt Crow stood in the doorway with the African grey parrot on her shoulder.

'Here at bleedin' last! Here at bleedin' last!'

'I take it that's your aunt,' said the driver with the roll-up, and as the wind whipped around them, Minerva caught the scent of something other than just tobacco.

She breathed in the earthy scent and smiled sweetly at the men, 'It certainly is, and that's Roger by the way. Didn't one of you say you knew my aunt?'

'I deliver her coal on a Monday,' said the second chap leaning against the front wheel of Mr. Morris, rolling up his own cigarette with great concentration. 'Always makes me a cuppa…'

Aunt Crow waved from the doorway, 'I'll put the kettle on…it's a bit cold out here!'

'Put the bloody kettle on! Put the bloody kettle on!'

'Roger, that's enough, you Goddess-forsaken bird! Come in when you're ready everyone, there's crumpets on the stove.'

The two men looked at each other and began to push Mr. Morris over to the house.

The distinct smell of animal was the first thing to strike Minerva as they entered the hallway of Spellstead, closely followed by the dilapidated, wooden sign swinging perilously across the door frame.

'Ouch!' Minerva clutched the side of her head as she ducked away from the sign, grateful for the numbing effect of the brandy and wondering how to avoid further injury over the next two weeks. She made a quick mental note to put a warning sign somewhere more obvious or to perhaps consume increased amounts of brandy to narrow the effects of any more pain. Either way, one or both would work...the important thing was to tell Isis, who was right behind her.

'Ouch! Oh ouch!'

Isis doubled up immediately to nurse her injury without realizing the dangling sign had taken her hairpiece with it.

Witnessing the scene in front of them, the two men sniggered loudly, which did them no favours as Roger so plainly put it:

'It'll get you next time you fuckers! Next time you fuckers! Next time you —'

'Shut it right now, Roger!' Aunt Crow shouted above the noise of a furiously bubbling kettle. 'The darn thing is supposed to turn off but it doesn't!'

Minerva and Isis stumbled their way past the ghostly apparition of Aunt Crow and through the steam, eventually finding a safe place to sit down while the two truckers followed, choking and gasping as Roger continued to herald them in:

'Steamy bastard windows, bastard windows!'

Minerva struggled to catch her breath, delving into her bag for something to remedy the situation. 'Isis, do you have the hag stone? I'm sure you had it earlier...'

'Did I?'

'Yes, you put it in your bag after I cast the spell, remember?'

Isis, began rummaging in her own bag and wailed, 'Oh dear, no!'

'What is it, Isis?'

'It's gone...through the holes!'

'What do you mean?' said Minerva, waving the steam away and thinking about how fuzzy it would make her hair. 'We know it had a *hole* in it, are you talking about a black hole?'

'No! I'm talking about the holes in my bag, it must be the silk, it frays very easily.'

'And it frays more when you fiddle about with it like you do, Isis. You're always fiddling with something! And now the hag stone's gone – my best little battery charger!'

The trucker's faces brightened when Aunt Crow shoved a plate of hot crumpets under their noses. 'Minerva, I shouldn't worry about a missing hag stone, you'll find plenty round here for magical purposes. Spellstead is the national grid for hag stones. It's positively crawling with them!'

Before Minerva had a chance to reply, there was a loud, snuffling sound accompanied by grunting and snorting from under the table.

'What's THAT?!' screamed Isis.

Minerva looked down to see what she thought at first was a fat dog, but on further inspection realized it must be Brenda the pot-bellied pig, hoovering the floor.

'*There* you are, Brenda,' said Aunt Crow with a sigh of relief, 'I did wonder when you were coming to say hello to everyone...and no better timing than just before I go. She's such an intelligent creature really – clears up and feeds herself at the same time – you won't find that in any other animal I can tell you. Pigs are smart!'

'A *pig*,' said Isis, struggling to keep her voice down, 'You didn't tell me anything about a pig, Minerva...in the house.'

'Oh yes, this is her home,' said Aunt Crow, stroking the broad and bristly back with a large grey feather. 'But like I told

Minerva, she's no trouble at all – very clean, considering – just sweep up once a day and that's it. Herself and Didge are no bother at all. You won't know they're here...'

'Didge?' said Isis, gripping onto the sides of her chair and peering under the table for what, she had no idea.

Minerva shuffled about in her chair and reached into her bag, hoping the brandy was in it. When she found it, she wasted no time in adding a large shot to her tea and without asking Isis, poured a generous amount into hers too.

'Now where did I see him last?' said Aunt Crow peering over her spectacles and around the room, 'Oh yes, he's over there look...in his favourite place by the stove. He feels the cold, don't you Didge dear?'

Minerva and Isis followed her gaze to the other side of the kitchen, where coiled up on an old threadbare rug, was a huge brown snake.

Minerva could feel a gasp from Isis as they picked up their cups together and gulped down the contents. It was one of those moments when words fail to even surface in the mind, let alone materialize verbally. It was also one of those moments when it's better not to say anything because every ounce of concentration is needed to hang on to the thin thread of sanity disappearing fast into the ether. Yes, it was definitely one of those moments when there's only one thing for it.

More brandy.

13

A Blast from the Past

Morrigan was growing into her name in more ways than one. Not only was she a bold and courageous little warrior, but also beginning to show real leadership qualities, especially with her animal friends.

She bossed the dogs around, the puppies in particular, telling them off when they sank their razor sharp teeth into her plump, soft skin. And in their games of rough and tumble, she took great delight in preparing her four-legged soldiers for battle and then watching the war play out between them.

When she wasn't leading the dog pack she was playing a gentler game with Lazarus and Crow Bird who now lived permanently together in Bob's old stable. Nothing excited her more than joining the pony and the bird for morning drills of herding into stable corners and the paddock outside while her mother mucked out. Combine a warrior toddler, a cunning bird and a tough little pony and you have a fearsome trio.

One dark and murky morning after the argument with Joe in the pub, Ronnie was in no mood for any noisy playfulness from the three musketeers and bundled them all into the small paddock for some peaceful mucking out time. Lazarus was especially good with Morrigan, and because Ronnie could see and hear them she was happy enough to part company with all three while she took out her anger from the night before, stabbing an imaginary Allan Key with a fork many times over.

She couldn't understand why some people paid a therapist money to feel the same sense of relief. Anger was such a primal and basic emotion, where was the sense in trying to manage it? Fire had to be worked out physically and released to the elements where it had come from, her mother had taught her that. *Suppressed anger is so unhealthy, Rhiannon!*

A bit of fury wasn't always a bad thing but she must speak to Joe tonight when she felt calmer. It had been too difficult last night. She hated rows and she hated what caused them even more. Allan Key for a start. Who did he think he was? Some puffed up drummer with *connections,* she'd heard that one before. It wouldn't have been so bad if Joe hadn't of been so happy, but it unnerved her. Joe said she was jealous but he'd been with the band, *his* band, for ages, *years* – and she'd never reacted like this before. But then, they'd never been on tour before.

She was deep in thought when the sound of Sophia's laughter and Morrigan's squeals of delight brought her back to the present. Smiling, she sidled over to the stable door and peeked out. Lazarus was walking quite calmly in a circle around the toddler who was waving a stick in the air like a sergeant major while Crow Bird danced up and down on the pony's rump, squawking loudly at the child.

Sophia laughed and called over to Ronnie, 'Roll up, roll up! Come and see the best show in town!'

As if on cue, all three performers became even more animated and Lazarus broke into a trot while the bird and Morrigan bobbed up and down together, squealing and squawking in delight. Ronnie stood watching, 'Looks like you got the front row seat while I'm up here in the gods!'

Sophia, still laughing, clapped and sang out at the top of her voice, 'Encore, encore!'

Morrigan proceeded to puff her little chest and run on the spot.

'If she carries on at this rate, she'll be heading for a nap soon after breakfast,' called Ronnie.

'At least that'll give you a bit of a break. But what a performance, eh Ron? I've never seen anything like it!'

'Yeah, she's a proper little drama queen, just like her grandmother!'

Sophia walked over to the stables in silence and stopped in the doorway, 'I don't suppose you've heard the latest have you?'

'What's that? I don't really see any of the others here to be honest. I quite like the fact we're tucked away in this little corner...'

Sophia nodded, 'I must admit, gossip is not my thing either, but it was Gail herself who I spoke to yesterday, when I went to the house to pay my livery.'

Without taking her eyes off her daughter and friends in the paddock, Ronnie half turned to Sophia, 'And what, pray tell is the *latest* then? Come on out with it...I'm in no mood for any suspense this morning!'

'Thought you were looking a bit pensive, everything okay?'

'Oh, just had a bit of a tiff with Joe last night, that's all.'

Sophia frowned. 'That's not like you two.'

'No it isn't, but throw the new drummer into the mix and everything changes doesn't it? Allan Key has a *band tour* up his sleeve. Honestly, he's so far up himself it's not true and what's worse is that Joe seems to be falling for it.'

'Oh I see,' said Sophia lowering her voice, 'Do you think it's anything worth worrying about though? I mean, it might not happen, or if it does, would it be that bad?'

Ronnie sighed, 'No, maybe not and maybe you're right, as usual. There I go, hurtling down a rabbit hole again!'

Sophia chuckled. 'Yeah, maybe hold fire on it for the time being, Ron. No crime committed yet as far as I can see. Anyway, Gail...'

'What did she say?'

Sophia ran a slender hand through her blonde hair. 'It's Gavin,' she said slowly, 'he's back from Oz.'

Ronnie glanced over at the paddock. 'Are you serious?'

'I'm dead serious. Gail's a pretty reliable source.'

Ronnie didn't argue with her. She'd trust the owner of the yard with her life, as she had on the day of the accident. Gail had literally come to the rescue out on the sea wall at the time. She'd answered Sophia's SOS call, sent for the ambulance and the vet and put blankets over Ronnie. And when the vet had arrived and Ronnie was carted off in the ambulance with Sophia, Gail had stayed with Bob in his final hours.

No one else had done that. But Gail had done it and she was grateful.

'Yes,' said Ronnie, 'Gail's as good a source as any I suppose. But Gavin, of all people!'

'I know, thought he'd gone for good didn't we?'

Ronnie looked across to the paddock again and managed a nervous laugh, 'Well it's only been a couple of years and a bit. But not long for someone who was planning a future out there!'

'Maybe it's only a holiday,' said Sophia with a serious look. 'Maybe he's earning such good money he could afford to take a break and come visit for a while. His mum still lives here after all.'

'Christ, I don't know what to think, it's a bit of a bloody shock. Did Gail say anything else? When did he get back? How did she find out?'

'Just a couple of days ago, she said. And Gail's good friends with his mum, that's how he got the farrier work here, remember? She had a horse at livery here some years ago now - bloody great Suffolk Punch it was – feet like dinner plates. No wonder he became a farrier, would've cost her a fortune to have him shod!'

Ronnie stared at her, '*Oh my god*, do you think Gail told her about me? About Morrigan? Do you think she knows? Because if she does, then she'll tell her son won't she? She'll tell Gavin and that'll be it. Sophia, what am I going to do?'

Sophia began walking over to the paddock, 'First off, calm bloody down Ron. Let's get this little lot in shall we? Has Lazarus had his breakfast yet?'

'Yes he had it first thing,' said Ronnie, 'I just need to fill a hay net for him.'

'Okay, you do that and I'll bring him and his entourage in and stick the kettle on and make a nice cuppa'. How's that sound?'

'It sounds better than what's going on in my head for a start.'

'Get on with that hay net, there's not a lot of grazing out here and your pony is probably hungry, not to mention your daughter who's chewing her fingers, and dirty fingers by the looks of them!'

'Don't give me more stress!' cried Ronnie from the hay shed.

Sophia's voice was firm, 'I'm just trying to get you to focus on priorities. It's a bit of a shock about Gavin, I know, but don't give your head too much to think about now. One thing at a time.'

'You're right, I know you're right,' said Ronnie trying to convince herself.

She looked down at the hay net she was filling and breathed in the scent of meadows and earth and thought of Bob. And as her breathing steadied and her mind slowed down she felt a velvety nose brush past her hand and warm air touch her face. 'Hello boy,' she muttered, 'I'm glad you're here.' And for a moment, all was well.

Animals know these things. They hear the sound of torment and worry, they know the inside of our hearts when they're hurting - they see the pain - and do what they can to take it away.

* * *

Sophia stood in the tack room doorway with Morrigan. 'You look like you've seen a ghost.'

'Maybe I have,' whispered Ronnie.

'Really?'

Morrigan ran to her mother and Ronnie swung her up into her arms and held her little body close. She smelt of malted milk biscuits, damp earth and baby wipes.

'It's Bob, he's right here, I can feel him. I know it sounds mad but...'

'It doesn't.'

Ronnie pulled Morrigan closer, 'You're not just saying that I hope.'

'Give me some credit, Ron, I'm not so insensitive to the finer details of life.'

Ronnie gave a soft laugh. 'Yeah, but this is taking things a bit further wouldn't you say?'

Sophia handed Ronnie a steaming mug before climbing onto a straw bale, 'Do you see him?'

'Not exactly, but I know it's him. The other week after we bought Lazarus back - when I was on my own in the stable with that poor pony not knowing whether he was going to make it - Bob came and I just knew.'

'That everything would be all right?'

'Completely. No question. I heard the munching and I saw the hay net move against the wall on its own. I saw it Sophia!'

'If that's what you saw, Ron, I believe you. I can understand why he'd show up.'

'You can?'

'Of course, it stands to reason. There was always something special between you and Bob. When you got upset about anything, he'd do that thing with his nose; letting you know he was there on your side. He was a good friend to you Ron, I saw it with my own eyes. He was an amazing animal…a healer.'

Ronnie's vision blurred as she fixed her eyes on the floor.

'Mummy cry,' said Morrigan, wiping a tiny hand across her cheek.

Without saying a word, Sophia opened her arms and Ronnie fell against her.

There is great comfort to be found in a silent hug.

* * *

Sophia watched Ronnie put a dozing Morrigan into her buggy,

'Feeling better?' she said softly, 'Must be reassuring having Bob around.'

Ronnie tucked the thick blanket tightly around her daughter's limp body, deep in thought. 'It's lovely to know he's here.'

'Always knew you were otherworldly!'

'Strange and weird you mean, like my mother.'

'You said it, not me!'

'But you were thinking it, be honest.'

'Rhiannon Crafty, you are your own worst enemy. When are you going to start believing in yourself for once? You have a gorgeous child and a great bloke, who adores you...'

'Possibly not for much longer now Gavin's back,' said Ronnie, biting her lip.

'Why should that make a difference to the way Joe feels about you? He's always known about Gavin, you never hid that from him. And he treats Morrigan like his own.'

'That's what worries me Sophia. It's not the fact that Joe isn't her father, but because Gavin *is!*'

'Hang on a minute, am I right in thinking Gavin doesn't *know* he's Morrigan's father, mainly because he buggered off to Australia well before she was born, saving you the trouble of telling him?'

Ronnie nodded, 'That's about right, yes. I never told him and as far as I know, neither has anyone else.' She stopped for a moment, her eyes widening like saucers, 'What if Gail *did* tell his mother?'

'Why would she do that? Did you ever tell Gail who the father was?'

Ronnie glanced at the sleeping child. 'No of course I didn't. No one knows, apart from you and my mother, David and Isis. That's about it, I think.'

'So where does Gavin's mother come into it? She doesn't even keep her horse here anymore! In fact it's probably well and truly in horsey heaven by now for sure. Gail just happened to mention she'd seen his mother and that's when she told me that Gavin was back! '

Ronnie clasped both hands either side of her head, 'Oh Jesus!'

Sophia took a deep breath in and out, 'You're confused because I mentioned Gail and Gavin's mother – only because that's how I found out – and NOT because either of them know the truth. Ron, I think we can assume your secret is safe.'

Ronnie rolled her eyes and ran her fingers through her thick, dark fringe, 'I bow, as usual, to your innate wisdom and powers of reason and logic, Sophia. You're a better man than me in the rationality department.'

'Oh come on Ron, it's not that difficult to work out, surely?'

'Maybe not for you, but for someone who's tired and emotional, it's a bit of a head banger.'

Sophia reached into her pocket and pulled out a squashed packet of malted milk biscuits. 'I think we need sugar.'

'Maybe the stronger kind,' said Ronnie, glancing at her mobile, 'like the liquefied, golden sort in a glass. The Old Druid's usually open by now...what d'ya reckon your honour? Are you up for a drop of Druid Fluid at such an unearthly hour?'

'I'd say at a time like this it would have to be compulsory. It's been a while since we indulged in such a decadent past time, what the hell, eh?'

Ronnie was up and pushing the buggy out of the tack room door, 'I was hoping you'd say that!'

'The Old Druid it is then,' said Sophia, popping a malted

milk into her mouth.

14

Flatulence and Feathers

Spellstead Hall took on an eerie silence after Aunt Crow had gone. When her taxi didn't show up, she was most grateful of a lift to the coach station with the truckers. 'How kind of you,' she called to the two men straining under the weight of a mountain of luggage, 'These things always happen for a reason, don't they? That taxi driver must have known you were here...why else would he not turn up? Don't call me unless something dies, Minerva...' she called behind her, 'There's a list on the table with all the necessary information...food and when to feed it, spells and when to apply if needed, plus the address of the travel company and cruise ship I'm on. Oh and Brenda is a nosey devil and a bit of a tea-leaf, so you might want to elevate anything worthy of her interest – which amounts to most things – out of her reach. See you on my return and enjoy Spellstead, it will grow on you I'm sure!'

Minerva looked at Isis and Isis looked at the table. There was no list. Only the empty plate where the crumpets had been, the purple teapot, half a jug of milk and a pot of sugar with some scattered teaspoons and cups.

'I can't see it can you?' said Isis, glancing around the untidy kitchen. All kinds of objects hung by hooks on the low wooden beams...pans and spoons of all sizes swayed together alongside bunches of dried flowers and herbs. Flour spilled in heaps on crowded worktops next to empty juice cartons, while half eaten packets of biscuits sat on shelves between old books and oddly shaped jars.

A mountain of unwashed dishes peeked its ugly head above the top of the huge butler sink in the corner and an empty bottle of washing up liquid lay on its side on the draining board. A trail of green slime oozed out of the bottle and down the outside of the cupboard doors, coagulating into a pool of thick, sticky mess on the flagstone tiles.

Isis followed the trail of green slime across the kitchen floor to the grunting pig who was eagerly hoovering up every crumb and drip in sight. The noisy creature eventually latched onto the thick and slimy trail until over the edge of the table, a bristly faced Brenda appeared. And before Isis could reach across to rescue the piece of crumpled paper which looked like the list; Brenda got there first...

With a loud grunt the pig jumped onto the chair with her front trotters, quickly followed by the rest of her. Diving across the table to the empty crumpet plate which she licked with a ravenous clip of her black tongue, she devoured the paper in seconds. Minerva and Isis watched in silence as the the all important list disappeared in front of them.

This was not meant to happen.

'Did you just see what I saw?' said Minerva.

'If you're talking about that pig on the table, yes,' said Isis mechanically.

'I've a feeling I will be calling Aunt Crow sooner rather than later.' growled Minerva.

'She said only to call her if something died,' said Isis, her hand flying to her mouth, 'Oh no, you can't. Minerva, you don't mean it, surely?'

'I wish I was made of sterner stuff but alas no, I couldn't do it. But by the Lady I damn well feel like it at the moment, don't you? That little beast has just eaten our set of instructions for everything we need to know and do while we're here. What the hell are we supposed to do now? Make it up as we go along?'

'So maybe we should ring Aunt Crow up and ask her to repeat to us what was on the list? That way we can write it down again and keep it somewhere Brenda can't reach.'

Minerva thought for a moment as she watched the pig hoover her way around the kitchen, making a bee line for anything else she could eat. Whether it was edible or not was debatable only to those who were not pigs. What did it matter if you were? Pigs were not in the least bit interested in the finer points of nutritional assessment.

'I have a better idea,' said Minerva, reaching across the table for her bag and getting out the brandy.

'Something to steady the nerves while you think about it?'

'Not for me, I'm thinking of Brenda.'

Isis felt for the missing hairpiece and tugged at her turquoise slingbacks instead, 'I don't think pigs are meant to have alcohol are they? It can't be good for them.'

Minerva chortled, 'Since when did a pig think about what was good for it or not? In case you hadn't noticed, so far Brenda has demonstrated in no uncertain terms, just how little she cares about what she eats and what she doesn't...did you see how she was following that trail of washing up liquid? That is a pig with no agenda other than to seek out and devour anything in its sight.'

'So what's the idea behind plying her with brandy?'

'To make her sick.'

Minerva poured out a large shot of the brandy into a small bowl. 'And hopefully, before she digests the rest of the contents in her stomach which contains—'

'— the list,' said Isis, 'But won't it be difficult to read once it's been consumed?'

She screwed her face up in disgust and watched Minerva trying to coax Brenda from the hallway, back into the kitchen.

'Come along Brenda, back in here if you please, I have something very tasty for you I can strongly recommend. Just the thing to wash down all the crap you've just eaten!'

Minerva tapped the side of the bowl and looked around. Spotting a half opened loaf of bread on the side she grabbed a couple of slices and held them out at arm's length to Brenda who was shuffling back towards the kitchen with a keen look of renewed interest if her twitching snout was anything to go by.

Wrapping her ankles tightly around each other on the bottom rung of her chair, Isis stared at the spectacle in a mixture of disbelief and disgust.

'Wash down the shit, wash down the shit…come on! Come on!'

Minerva and Isis jumped as Roger called out from his cage in the hallway.

'Shut up you uncouth bird!' screamed Minerva while Isis covered her ears with both hands. 'Your assistance is not required!'

The high pitched squawking echoed around the kitchen in the most offensive manner. It was enough to threaten the sanity of any calm and normal person let alone the frazzled nerves of Isis, and Minerva's rapidly diminishing patience.

'Brenda and brandy…Brenda and brandy!' cried Roger, much to Minerva's dismay.

'How has he picked that up so quickly? I've hardly said a word.'

'You did mention both words…'

'Yes, but only a minute ago,' snapped Minerva. 'Be careful what you say Isis, we don't want our secrets leaking out to all and sundry by the coarse and mindless twitterings of that bird. Now come on Brenda…that's it, follow me…this way…look what we have for you!'

It was all too tempting for Brenda and much slurping began as Minerva stood over the pig, poised with the brandy bottle, quick to add more as she finished each round. Isis watched in silence, hands wringing with the rest of her body's contortions as she wriggled and wobbled about on her chair. As quickly as the brandy glugged from the bottle to the bowl and into Brenda, her bristly snout poked into the air looking for a refill. Eventually Minerva gave up pouring the drink into the bowl and instead tipped it straight down Brenda's throat.

Isis wasn't sure whether to laugh or cry. The greedy pig seemed to be enjoying the hand feeding, and as her bristly sides bellowed in and out, Minerva pulled the bottle away and waited. 'Can you fetch another bowl Isis?'

'You're not going to give her any more are you?'

'Not if I can help it. This, with a bit of luck will be the vomit bowl and the answer to our problem.'

Isis hesitated before wobbling off her chair to seek out

another bowl. She placed a large cake bowl in front of Brenda, who sniffed and snorted in disgust when she realized it was empty. 'She doesn't look like a sick pig to me,' said Isis, not really sure what a sick pig looked like, 'I know we haven't known her very long but she doesn't look any different than when we first met her, Minerva. Although come to think of it, she does seem more relaxed now.'

'She's had a bellyful of brandy, Isis, and one doesn't consume the amount she has without consequences. I've never seen anyone or anything put away that amount of booze so quickly, I can only assume and *hope* that it will all come back in the same manner. Stand by Isis and out of the line of fire if you can, those sling backs maybe a hit on the dance floor but I doubt they're waterproof.'

Isis glanced down at her turquoise sandals and again at Brenda before stepping back onto something large and brown. Before she had time to realize what it was it had slid off, gathering speed as it made its way towards the door and out into the hall.

'Ye' gods that was Didge,' said Minerva catching her breath and craning her neck in the direction of the snake's slippery exit, 'He's a smooth operator if ever I saw one. Never said a word did he?'

Isis squealed and jumped onto the table in one awkward leap, 'Are you serious? I never heard it…'

'Isis, when will you stop taking me so literally? Of course they can't talk, it was a figure of speech! What I *meant* was, you wouldn't have known he was there would you?'

'No I didn't…at all.'

'Exactly,' sighed Minerva, 'How your nerves are going to get through this next week I don't know. But one thing I do know;

Brenda will not be the only one consuming copious amounts of this stuff.'

She raised the brandy bottle just as Brenda produced a belch so loud it made the teaspoons buzz on the table and the teapot quiver. With mouths open, Minerva and Isis stared at the pig who belched again and with sides bellowing slumped hard onto the floor before lifting her wispy tail to pass another blast of wind.

The series of gaseous explosions from both ends of Brenda was not only loud and intrusive to the ear but the assault on their noses was something Minerva and Isis could never have imagined. The coughing and spluttering which followed, accompanied by much waving of arms and bursts of laughter, was the result of shock and amusement in equal measures.

Meanwhile, Brenda had managed to recover enough to a standing position where she swayed one way and then the other, belching and farting continuously. Minerva didn't know whether to keep her hands on her ears or hold her nose while Isis attempted an odd combination of both.

And Roger shrieking from the hallway didn't help: 'Who's farted you stinky bastard? Stinky bastard! Stinky bastard!'

'Did we bring any incense?' gasped Minerva, struggling for breath.

'I think I packed some…shall I have a look and see?'

'Yes do Isis, please. I'm not sure how much longer I can stand this assault on my nasal passages. I've smelt some things in my day, but by the Lord and Lady's bog roll holder, I have never smelt anything like Brenda's arse, have you?'

Peeling away the chiffon collar from her red and patchy neck Isis finished her latest bout of coughing, 'I can't say that I have, no. It's quite the most awful smell ever, in fact *smell* is almost too good a word for it.'

'You're right,' said Minerva, pressing the corner of her sleeve hard against her right nostril.

Isis was glad to get out into the hallway where she began to rummage among the pile of bags beside Roger and his cage.

'Brandy and Brenda! Brandy and Brenda! You stinky bastard…you stinky bastard!'

'Oh please, Roger, that's quite enough!' said Isis from the inside of a large carpet bag, 'You need to curb that tongue - no, *beak,* of yours – it's most offensive. I don't know how Aunt Crow has put up with you all these years!'

The loud farting noise which followed caused Isis to look round only to discover no one else was there but Roger, urgently bobbing up and down on his perch and flapping his wings. She dug her hands deeper into the bag and tried to concentrate on the slim box of incense sticks she knew were there but with Roger's farting in her ears, it wasn't easy.

She thought of Gerald's smooth voice and brown body, and smiled. It was a coping strategy which worked until Minerva's voice rang out from the kitchen, 'Any luck out there Isis? It's suffocating in here!'

Isis rummaged faster until finally she came upon the incense. Stumbling back into the kitchen, she handed the box to a retching Minerva…one hand clasped over her mouth and nose and a lighter in the other. Poor Brenda was still passing wind from both ends and slowly making her way around the room, rooting with her snout in a continued and unrelenting quest for more food.

Minerva finally lit the incense and as *Faeries in the Forest* wafted around the table it went a small way to lighten the atmosphere and mask the hideous smell. Sliding a cup of brandy across the table, Minerva managed a weak grin. 'Get that down you, Isis. It may help to eliminate or at least dilute the intensity of the past half an hour.'

Isis raised her head and peered at Minerva from a clump of spiky, copper hair. She took the glass and said nothing, knocking back the contents in one hearty swig.

'Your hairpiece,' said Minerva, 'Where is it? I'm sure it was there earlier.'

Isis looked puzzled and felt the top of her head. 'Yes it was, and I have no idea where it can be.'

'You must have caught it on something. What about that broken sign hanging in the doorway? I bumped my head on it coming in, and you were right behind me.'

'Was I?' said Isis wearily, 'I'll take a look later, when I've got my breath back.'

Minerva flew out of the kitchen and down the hall, glad of an excuse to remove herself from the fumes of fairies and farts in the kitchen. Heading towards the dangling Spellstead sign, she approached Roger's cage where all was unusually quiet.

Finding it hard to believe how a bird like Roger could have changed in such a short space of time, she peeked through the bars and saw why. There, on top of the bird's head was the copper hairpiece. Carefully preening his feathers and clearly not wanting to dislodge his new attire, Roger perched in silence.

'Well I never,' hissed Minerva through the bars, 'I'm not sure what Isis will say to this but it certainly seems to have shut you up. Who'd have thought a new hair style could have such an effect?'

Roger crept sideways along the perch towards the nosy human and puffed his grey feathers up and out as much as he could manage without losing his new robe. Squawking quietly, he tapped the bars with his beak and let out the loudest farting noise.

'You are the bloody limit, you god forsaken vilest of birds. In fact bird is too good a description for one so deprived!' She stopped herself from shaking the cage but held onto the corners and shut her eyes as he bellowed out another one of Brenda's farts inches from her ears.

Stomping back to the kitchen with her ears ringing, Minerva's mind began to wander in all kinds of directions, not one of them involving Roger's survival. By the time she got back to the kitchen, she had committed in her mind every form of parrot torture and abuse known to man.

'I'm sure it will be easier than you think,' she said to Isis, rubbing the inside of her ears and pouring herself a large brandy.

'What will?' said Isis to the fuzzy frame in front of her.

'Killing Roger,' spat Minerva, 'One of us has to go, Isis, and it's not me. I promised Aunt Crow I'd look after the place and I'm not shirking my responsibilities.'

Isis screwed her face up at Minerva, 'Then you can't kill Roger can you? He's been with her forever and you have a responsibility to him as well.'

'After his latest performances, do you really think I care about his welfare? He has absolutely no respect or thought for anyone but himself. I've never come across such deliberate rudeness in an animal. He's got to go!'

Isis pulled herself up from the table and tried to level with Minerva's beetroot face, 'Look Minerva, it's all been a bit hectic today, the last few hours particularly, how about we turn in for the night and get some sleep? Things will look different in the morning.'

'That doesn't work I'm afraid Isis, you know me better than that. There are still certain things to sort out - the list for a start!'

'How can we sort it out if Brenda won't bring it up? We've tried and she won't be sick, it's not going to happen…'

'Then I shall have to ring Aunt Crow.'

'Surely it can wait until the morning? None of the animals are going to starve before then are they? And besides, I'm sure if we searched around and thought about it we could work out for ourselves what they eat.'

Minerva looked at Isis, 'That'll be cyanide pills for that damn parrot, then.'

Isis couldn't imagine where the cyanide pills would come from and didn't want to even think about it, 'Did you find my hairpiece?'

'Are you ready for this? Roger is wearing it of all things, can you believe that? The audacity of it! Go and look for yourself if you don't believe me.'

Isis had to bite her lip, it was the only way she could stifle the nervous laughter threatening to erupt. She got up slowly and with Minerva following close behind, ventured out into the dark hallway once again.

As they reached the cage, all was quiet as Isis peered through the bars. 'Are you sure you didn't let him out? I can't see him.'

'Of course I didn't let him out,' said Minerva, hovering over her shoulder.

Peering closer into the cage, they cried out together. Even in the dim light it was obvious that Roger was not on his perch, in fact he was very much off it.

'He's not moving,' said Isis, not moving either.

'No he's not,' said Minerva, 'And you know why that is, don't you?'

'He's not —'

'—Dead? It certainly looks that way.'

'How do you know for sure?' Isis turned to look at Minerva, 'You didn't did you?'

'What do you mean?'

'You were only talking about it a minute ago!' said Isis, looking horrified.

'Yes I know, but that doesn't mean I killed him does it? What, you really think I'd do that Isis. Are you mad?'

Isis was beginning to wonder. 'You didn't do it then?'

Minerva stepped back from the cage and glared at Isis, 'How the hell was that going to happen Isis? If you recall, I was backwards and forwards with Brenda and brandy, fairies and forests, and farting! How could I have done it?'

'So you didn't mean what you said?'

Minerva fixed her gaze firmly ahead. 'You know me, Isis, it was a spur of the moment thing and it appears much the same has happened to Roger,' she gestured towards the copper hairpiece. 'It's clearly a case of natural causes.'

'You think so?' said Isis, staring at the bottom of the cage.

'It's obvious, can't you see?'

All Isis could see was Roger's grey and red plumes beneath a mound of copper hair. She stared back at Minerva, her eyes like saucers as her hand flew to the top of her head.

'I'm afraid so, Isis, strangled and suffocated by his own fair feathers.'

'And my hair!'

'Don't be ridiculous, it's not your fault. It just happened to be there, that's all.'

'Yes, but...'

'Stop right there, Isis. If you want to split hairs...' she stifled a grin, 'then you could blame the sign which claimed your hairpiece in the first place and all manner of things before it...but it's happened, it's not your fault and that's it'.

Isis stared at Minerva in disbelief, 'You don't think he did it on purpose do you?'

'By fair means or foul, this parrot is dead. No question about it, he has gone to join his feathered friends in the Summerlands.'

'We must give him a decent send off,' said Isis in deep thought.

'First things first, there's Aunt Crow,' said Minerva, feeling the beginnings of a cold sweat, 'How am I going to tell her?'

'You'll have to ring her, and soon.'

'Why so soon? Why spoil her holiday before it's begun? Surely it makes more sense to wait until it's over, that'll give us time to work out what to say. It stands to reason.'

Isis couldn't see the rhyme or reason in any of it. 'So what are we going to *do* with him until she gets back?'

'Nothing,' said Minerva quite adamantly. 'He stays where he is until further notice.'

'Won't he start to smell?'

'Not as badly as Brenda and her exploding backside, that's for sure.'

'I'll take your word for it,' murmured Isis.

'Good. That's settled then. Now I don't know about you Isis, but I could do with a nightcap, something to soothe the turbulent waters of this unknown territory we find ourselves in. What about you?'

'Now that you put it like that, I don't see why not,' said Isis, reaching inside the cage for the missing hairpiece and placing it back on her head.

'Good. That's decided then,' said Minerva, wrinkling her nose at the musty air in the hallway.

The faeries in the forest had vanished…leaving the stagnant traces of Brenda's flatulence and Roger's remains floating in the ether.

15

Frozen Stiff

Gerald looked up at the church as he wandered across the village green. The thick wooden door creaked heavily as he pushed it open and stepped inside. He wasn't looking for salvation or solace, or even shelter…a church was just a building to Gerald. Who was inside it was much more interesting.

'Ah, there you are,' his words echoed across the pews, 'I thought I might find you here.'

David looked up from the front row where he was playing his guitar. 'Gerald,' he mused, 'good to see you…just having a bit of a practice.'

'You couldn't have chosen a better place,' said Gerald, looking around at the stone walls, 'such wonderful acoustics!'

David stood the guitar carefully against the altar and gestured to Gerald to come and sit down. 'Care for a cuppa? We have all mod cons here, you know…'

A few minutes later, with mugs of tea and a plate of custard creams between them the two men sat in comfortable silence. Neither felt the need to fill the gap, until Gerald caught sight of two angels in bright gold stitching on a prayer cushion. 'Have you heard from Minerva?' he said, brushing off crumbs from his gardening cords.

'Funny you should say that, I was just about to ask you the same question about Isis. No, I haven't heard a word to be honest, not that it's unusual for Minerva. She tends to become quite immersed in whatever she's doing and I'd imagine they've got their hands full where they are.'

'Yes,' said Gerald, 'by the sounds of it, this Aunt Crow has quite a menagerie of animals. The parrot for a start…it's not every day you come across one with Tourette's is it?'

David laughed. 'No, but don't you think most parrots who were given a free rein would develop those kinds of tendencies anyway?'

'I don't know about that,' pondered Gerald over a custard cream, 'Wouldn't it depend on the company? He's an old hand at it according to Isis, been with Minerva's aunt a long time. Old familiars are the best.'

'Is that so?' said David. 'I seem to remember my grandmother being very fond of a particular rabbit she kept as a pet.'

'Ah, you see…there's no separating a wise woman from her familiars,' said Gerald. 'Was your grandmother a religious woman, church abiding?'

'She attended church from what I can remember, but as I told Minerva, she did have a set of tarot cards, which my grandfather the local pastor, frowned upon. She would wait until he was reading someone's bands and then she would get her cards out and read fortunes with them. It was all very dark and mysterious but I was always fascinated by them. The images were deeply mystical to me, so it seems very synchronistic that now, after all these years, I should meet someone like Minerva doing just what my grandmother did.'

Gerald let out a deep chuckle. 'Does doing what *you* do ever come between you?'

'It hasn't yet and I don't see why it should, Minerva and I have a mutual understanding...but there *is* someone who will have a problem with it, I'm sorry to say.'

Gerald raised his eyebrows.

'It's my mother who's coming over for a visit soon...she's a committed member of the church.'

'You mean she's a staunch Catholic.'

It was more of a statement than a question, but David didn't mind.

'She is indeed, Gerald. And to be perfectly honest with you, I can't say I'm looking forward to it. Of course she's my mother and I have every respect for her but she can be difficult at times. And as far as Minerva is concerned,well...'

'Two strong women eh?' said Gerald, 'And one a Witch, too? Fancy getting yourself mixed up with one of her kind, father!'

David spluttered over his tea. 'Hmm, I'll be the rose between two thorns won't I? Thank the lord it's only for a few days.'

Gerald chuckled into his tea, 'Light the blue touch paper and stand well back! In fact the fireworks will be just on time with November the 5th just around the corner. Great timing, I'd say.'

'Would you?' said David, the beginnings of a smile flitting across his face. 'We shall see. I'm under no illusion that they're going to get on but I do hope they can at least find some common ground between them. It will certainly help things along.'

'Isn't it obvious?' said Gerald. 'They already have that

common ground between them - you! And if they can't sort their differences out for themselves then surely they can do it out of respect for your good self.'

'Ah yes,' chortled David, 'in an ideal world we'd all get on wouldn't we, Gerald? But unfortunately, human nature isn't always the most accommodating of things and people are people. And although we can speculate about my mother and Minerva, the truth of the situation will only become apparent when they meet. Who knows what will happen but I can tell you one thing for sure, I am not going to lose any sleep over it.'

'Sounds like the right attitude,' said Gerald, folding his arms.

'It's the *only* attitude,' said David picking up his guitar again, 'Why put yourself through hell before the event? Spending too much time dwelling on what hasn't happened yet is the perfect breeding ground for anxiety in my book.'

'Indeed.' said Gerald, his gaze wandering to the huge bible sitting on the altar. 'I'm all for staying in the present moment. I'm sure Minerva and Isis will return refreshed and relaxed after their break away. It'll do them good.'

'I'm sure you're right Gerald. A proper *girly* time away usually does the trick doesn't it? Women seem to benefit greatly by spending quality time together, and in such a wonderful place by the sounds of it.'

'Yes, Spellstead Hall will be working its magic upon them, no doubt,' said Gerald, looking up as a passing cloud darkened the stained glass windows.

* * *

Minerva stared at the yellowing piece of paper in her hand. 'By the gods, I think we may have struck a bit of luck, Isis.'

Studying the spidery handwriting, she mouthed her findings with great concentration.

'I didn't think you believed in luck,' mumbled Isis on a mouthful of toast. 'You always say it's worse than the chaos theory and general randomness.'

'Let's call it synchronicity then, just to be on the safe side,' said Minerva, 'or I. Stuffham to be precise.'

'Who's that?'

'According to this, the local taxidermist,' said Minerva, shoving the paper between Isis and her slice of toast. 'Just what we're looking for wouldn't you say?'

Isis spluttered on a mouthful of tea. 'Are we?'

'Did you put brandy in that?'

'No! It's only breakfast time.'

'Yes, and don't we know it,' Minerva wrinkled her nose up at Brenda, happily foraging and farting around the kitchen. 'Anyway, back to business,' she said, waving Ivan Stuffham in the air, 'I think this man's skills are just what we need, considering...'

'You mean with Roger,' said Isis, glancing nervously down the hallway.

'That's right, a taxidermist is the answer to our problem Isis, albeit temporarily of course, that is until Aunt Crow realizes what her failing eyesight has tricked her into and discovers the cold, hard truth.'

'Minerva, am I hearing this right? You are proposing to get Roger stuffed, and leave him in his cage as if he were still alive?!'

'That's about the long and the short of it Isis, yes. Quite in-genius don't you think?'

'Can I ask, why Aunt Crow would have the need for a

taxidermist anyway?'

'You obviously haven't noticed the *collection* around the house.'

The truth was, Isis had avoided looking too closely at anything over the past twenty four hours – thanks to her brandy fuelled brain fog and the traumatic turn of events – and this had suited her. She didn't need to face any more stuffed animals in dark corners.

'N-n-no,' stuttered Isis, 'I hadn't noticed at all, actually. I was very tired last night when we turned in and it *was* late.'

'My favourite is the black sheep on the landing upstairs,' said Minerva, 'Odd little thing with three legs, if you look closely enough. At first I didn't see it - the leg that is, or rather the leg that *isn't* – because of the poor lighting. But then once the eyes get used to the dark, it's obvious.'

'How can you see something that's not there?' said Isis, looking baffled.

'That's exactly it, Isis. The mind plays tricks doesn't it? You think something's there because you're expecting it to be – a four-legged animal has four legs, normally…'

'Unless it's a three-legged black sheep'.

'Quite,' snapped Minerva, 'So I'm deducing from this that dear Aunt Crow likes to keep her familiars close to her, which is good news for Roger, don't you think?'

'Is it?'

Isis couldn't see how anything would be good news for Roger other than a miracle at this point, but Minerva was adamant.

'Of course it is, Isis. It means he will live on at Spellstead with Aunt Crow forever. I'd say that will soften the blow considerably and it also means that there's no time to waste. I must get in contact with Ivan Stuffham, pronto. We don't want Roger going past his best now do we?'

Isis wrinkled her nose. 'I can't imagine what that would look *or* smell like.'

'We needn't concern ourselves too much with that at the moment as I've made a temporary arrangement which should suffice for now,' said Minerva, picking up the telephone. 'Oh and Isis, would you mind giving Didge his breakfast? It's on the draining board and perhaps get a few more out of the freezer for later while you're at it? And I'll get onto Mr. Stuffham.'

Isis looked warily at Minerva and tried to ignore the feeling of dread creeping up over her. 'Erm, what is his breakfast exactly?'

She soon wished she hadn't asked as Minerva crossed the kitchen floor to the draining board and held aloft a small pink body. 'This, dear Isis, is a defrosted mouse, which, according to an old shopping list I happened to come across, is Didge's main diet. There are others in the freezer, to be given as and when.'

Isis could feel the contents rising up from her stomach but made a valiant attempt towards the freezer in the utility room next door and away from the poor pink and shrivelled creature on the draining board. As she lifted up the heavy lid of the old chest freezer, the gush of frosty air was not the only thing to shock her senses: 'Oh my god!' she cried, as the lid slipped from her grasp and landed with a dull thud.

Minerva stood frowning in the doorway with her hands on her hips. 'What *now*, Isis?' she barked, 'Anyone would think you'd seen a ghost!'

Isis stood shaking with one hand over her mouth and the other leaning heavily on the clamped down freezer lid. 'That's because I have,' she garbled, '…Roger.'

'Oh him, yes. I thought it best to keep him fresh until the taxidermist gets here.'

'In the freezer?'

Minerva waved Isis out of the way and lifted up the freezer lid. And there was Roger, the unmistakable red and grey plumage crunched down flat in a see-through plastic bag. 'Perfectly preserved, you see,' she said proudly, 'And lying in state until further notice, along with these little mites...' She picked up a parcel of newspaper and unwrapped it, taking a handful of tiny pink and frozen bodies with one hand while closing the lid of the freezer with the other. The thud went right through Isis and she clamped her eyes shut, half hoping and wishing she could disappear with the contents of the freezer into another world, like Narnia. 'Minerva, I don't feel too well.'

'I can see that,' said Minerva, brushing past her briskly, 'But really Isis, we don't have time to be giving in to weakness and woe. You're going to have to buck up and pull yourself together, that's all there is to it, I'm afraid. So there are dead things around the place, maybe more than you are used to seeing on average, but you need to face up to these old fears. Death can't hurt you!'

Isis tried to straighten up. 'Do you have any rescue remedy on you?'

Minerva gave a smug grin, 'No, but I have something better, my own version.'

She disappeared into the kitchen and reappeared almost instantly with a small brown bottle. Removing the lid, she handed it to Isis. '*Wake Me Up Before You Go, Go* is just the thing, believe me. The perfect magical remedy for anything which has reduced one to a blithering wreck. Get it down you, or rather up you would be more accurate. Look, like this...'

Squashing a nostril down with one finger, Minerva shoved the neck of the tiny bottle up the other nostril and breathed in deeply. Isis watched in quiet fascination as Minerva's cheeks flushed a dark crimson and her eyes got bigger. After repeating the process three times, she stopped suddenly.

'What's in that?' asked Isis, mesmerized.

'Horehound, picked by the light of the full moon and dried for a full cycle of thirteen moons, grounded and mixed with vervain and voila! There you have your magical wake up call.'

She inhaled again deeply from the tiny bottle before passing it to Isis who gingerly took it and repeated the operation. It seemed to work, because almost instantly she felt a charge of electricity run through her body and jumped to attention in front of Minerva.

'Now where were we?' frowned Minerva, marking time like a soldier, 'Ah yes, Didge's breakfast. These little creatures will need defrosting, and meanwhile you can give him the one on the draining board when you find him.'

'What do you mean, when I find him? Don't tell me I have to go and *look* for him,' panted Isis. 'He's not like Brenda, then?'

Minerva shook her head. 'No he isn't. Apart from when we first arrived, where he showed up in the kitchen, I haven't seen him since. Which means he has slithered off into the dark crevices of Spellstead of which I'd imagine, there are many. Snakes are slippery characters in more ways than one, but don't worry, you'll find him sooner or later.'

Isis helped herself to some more Wake Me Up Before You Go, Go before pushing it back into Minerva's hand and taking off on her newly appointed mission. Meanwhile, Minerva laid out the crumpled piece of paper on the table and proceeded to dial the number of the taxidermist.

After what seemed like an age, a faint and distant voice crackled onto the line and Minerva cleared her throat. 'Hello, is that Mr. Stuffham?'

'Mr. who?' came the faint reply.

'Mr. Ivan Stuffham, the taxidermist. Is that you?'

'Taxidermist, yes, that is correct. But you mis-pronounce my name.'

Minerva tried to place the foreign accent. 'Oh, I'm sorry about that Mr. err?'

'Stuffham with an 'oo', you understand 'yah? Am I making myself clear?'

'I think so…that's an 'oo' and not 'uh' is that right?'

'Is better yes. What is it can I do for you?'

'Well, I'm calling from Spellstead Hall, my Aunt's place. You've done some work in the past for her, I believe?'

There was a pause along the crackling line while Minerva waited, turning over the paper in her hand.

'You mean Lady Crow is it?'

'Yes!'

He laughed. 'Ah, but I have known Lady Crow for many years, and many times I have worked for her.'

Minerva dragged a sweating hand through her matted hair. 'Well, I'm glad about that, because I'm looking after Spellstead while she's on holiday.'

'Ah yes, I am seeing now. Very much she was looking forward to going away. And you are the keeper of the fort, yes?'

'I am, yes. I'm Aunt Crow's niece, Minerva.'

'Then everything is okay? No?'

Minerva swallowed hard for a second and glimpsed across to the utility room, 'Well, yes everything *was* okay until Roger the parrot died.'

'Oh,' he was silent. 'Does your aunt know?'

Minerva bit her lip, 'No she doesn't, yet. But she will…soon.'

After a slight delay, a very formal sounding Mr. Stuffham crackled back, 'I will see you in the next few days, goodbye.'

Minerva looked at the handset as it clicked to silence. 'Goodbye yourself, Mr. Stuffham.'

Just as she was replacing the handset on the window sill, she spotted a hag stone right beside it. She grabbed the ugly looking stone and rubbed it slowly between thumb and fingers, enjoying the bumps and curves and smoothness of the flint. Sometimes when life knocked the stuffing out of you, things came along to put it back. Things like bits of paper and taxidermists.

Minerva silently thanked the gods for reversing the wheel of fortune and began to hum loudly while she washed up, only hearing the cries from above when the clattering of pots and pans was over.

'Oh Isis,' she said, throwing down the purple marigolds and bolting upstairs, 'What now?!'

16

On the Cards

Ronnie walked slowly back from the muck heap, zig-zagging the wheelbarrow through the mud. She was glad of some time to sort out the mess going on in her head, not helped by a hangover, and she was better off at the stables, out in the fresh air and close to nature. And Bob.

She went over the row with Joe earlier and it pained her. It wasn't good to leave an argument unresolved but he had to go to work and she had to drop Morrigan off and get to the yard. There was never a right time for these things.

She recalled his face.

Joe never scowled or looked unhappy but he had been both in such a short space of time. How had she made him so unhappy, so quickly? She played it over in her mind like a bad film.

'You're going then?' had been her reply to his casual mention of a band tour over breakfast.

'Of course I'm going Ron. The *band's* going and it's my band, remember?'

'I'm not stupid, Joe.'

'Sometimes I wonder, Ron. You know the score, how many

more times do we have to go over it for god's sake?'

She wasn't used to him raising his voice, but she couldn't stop herself. Maybe it was the cider still talking, Sophia and herself had enjoyed quite a session in the Old Druid the day before.

Joe searched her tired face. 'Oh, I get it now…maybe we can try again once you're done with that hangover. Might be the best thing, eh?'

'It's not as if I go out that much at all now, in fact I *never* go out any more!'

'I'm not criticizing,' said Joe in a softer tone, 'I'm glad you've picked up again with Sophia, you go back a long way. And that's my point Ron - the band's been together a long time - we're like a family. It's what happens in bands.'

'And *Allan's* just jumped on the *band*-wagon, how convenient for him!' scoffed Ronnie.

Joe laughed. 'Nice pun! Oh come on, you know it's not like that. He's just a nice bloke who happens to be a bloody good drummer with some good connections, and genuinely wants to help us out.'

'I wouldn't flatter yourself too much,' she sneered. 'Wants to help *himself* out more like, Allan has his own agenda Joe! Don't ask me how, I just know it.'

'You've got him wrong there, where are you getting all this from?'

'Mamma coat, my coat!' cried a small voice.

Morrigan's face beamed up at Ronnie as the coat toppled from her grasp. Watching her wobble towards her, Ronnie's heart softened and grabbing the toddler and Land Rover keys she headed for the deck without a word. Joe called out behind her, 'Bye bye Mogs, and have a good day Rhiannon, the fresh air will do you good!'

She'd regretted not saying goodbye but stubbornness had stopped her. Backing down wasn't her style, especially with such an obvious thing. Couldn't he see the cracks with Allan forming right before his eyes like she could? Trouble was, Joe had a stubborn streak too and this was something he was standing his ground with.

Love could be blind. But in this case, thought Ronnie, it's *band* blindness.

He was right about one thing though, the fresh air was just what she needed. She breathed in the damp earthiness all around her and ambled back to the stables, not seeing the figure at first in the cloud of early morning mist.

'Hello Ronnie.'

The voice startled her and leaning towards the shrouded figure she tried to make out who it was. It couldn't be Joe, the stubbornness was still wedged fresh and firmly between them, she could feel it. No, it wasn't Joe, but the male voice was familiar.

'How's it going?'

The subtle hint of Australian drawl billowed into the frosty air and she stopped in front of the figure, putting the wheelbarrow down between them.

She could see him now. 'Gavin. What are you doing here?'

'Came to say hello, that's all.'

He seemed as tongue tied as she was and shuffled from one foot to the other, digging his hands deep into his pockets, the waxy scent of his jacket hanging between them.

'You're back then,' she said, not knowing what to say.

He laughed quietly, 'I'm back, yeah. Just got off the last spaceship over there.' He signalled to the light behind the muck heap.

She followed his hand as it pointed to the misty beyond and smiled. 'You might as well have done, it's not such an unimaginable thing. Weirder things have happened around here you know.'

'Is that right? What kind of things?'

Ronnie turned and glanced into the stable beside her. 'Dead things mostly.'

Gavin's dark eyes peered at her and she caught the waxy scent once again, reminding her of years before...the stable party, a lot of cider and writhing around at the back of the hay barn. It was strange how the senses could unlock the memories of the past.

'Who died?'

Her gaze swept to the ground and fixed on the uneven cracks in the concrete and she tried to hold her breath steady. 'You didn't hear about Bob?'

'No I didn't.'

She spoke quickly, 'We had an accident out on the sea wall, a fox hole brought us down and...'

Her voice trailed off and Gavin nodded. 'Sorry to hear that Ronnie,' his voice faltered, 'but you've got a new recruit I see.' He gestured to Lazarus, munching his hay in the stable.

'Yeah, this little fella is the one who came back from the dead.'

'A rescue?'

She nodded. 'From the marshes a few weeks ago. He was in a bit of a sorry state but he's pulled through and is doing good so far.'

'Good work,' said Gavin and paused, 'You always had a way with animals.'

'Did I?'

She regretted the words as soon as she said them. This was going on far too long.

'Yeah, you were different to the others here, most of them treating their horse like some fashion accessory. Not you though.'

'Bob was much more than that.'

'I know.'

Ronnie began to fidget. 'Anyway, you never said why you came back. Holiday?'

'Well, kind of, but Mum's not good. She's been crook for a while and I thought I should be here.'

'Oh, is it bad?'

'Bad enough. Cancer.'

The lack of emotion in his voice was not lost on Ronnie. She felt a pang of sadness remembering how Eve had suffered and how Joe had closed himself off for a long time afterwards. Losing a mother so young was a tough call.

She reached out and touched his arm. 'Christ, I'm sorry Gavin.'

He didn't say anything but sighed as her hand caught his arm. 'She's pretty crook, Ron, and you just don't know how long do you?'

Ronnie searched his face, noticing how sadness had changed him. 'None of us know how much longer we have, Gavin…one of life's mysteries I guess. All we can do is make the most of our time and spend it with the people who are important to us.'

'Yeah, doesn't take much working out really, does it?' He looked up at her, 'It's nice seeing you Ronnie, you're looking well. I'd better go.'

He stepped towards her, and before she could move, kissed her cheek. The warmth of him against her cold skin was comforting somehow and she did nothing to resist it.

'Nice to see you too Gavin,' she called after him as he turned away quickly. 'Drop by again, if you're around.'

There was a silence as he continued to walk. 'Gail's a good friend of Mum's so I'll be here again for sure. See you later.'

The sound of his boots crunched on the gravel as she watched him fade back into the early morning mist. The way he walked reminded her of Morrigan's toddling gait, which unnerved her, just as the slump of his broad shoulders saddened her. She didn't want to feel sorry for him, but she did. She didn't want to feel anything, but she couldn't help it.

* * *

Going about the rest of her stable duties in quiet contemplation, the mixture of emotions bubbled inside Ronnie and played on her mind. She needed to sit down and pulling her mobile from her pocket, called the one person she could think of who might be able to help. It was an age before anyone answered, by which time she was fully engrossed in the straw bale she was sitting on, absently plucking at the golden stalks.

'Ronnie darling, is everything okay?'

Her mother's sleepy voice immediately brought her back to the present. 'Yeah, I'm all right Mum, are you?'

After a slight hesitation, Minerva picked her words carefully, 'Apart from this rather rude awakening, I'm fine. But you're not.'

'Mum, do you have your cards handy? I could do with some guidance.'

She pulled out some loose strands of straw and placed them neatly beside each other, finding comfort in their order of appearance.

'One moment, let me get them…'

Ronnie waited, laying each piece of straw into a pattern and without thinking she realized she had made the shape of a pentacle.

'Can you hear me Ron? I've got you on loud speaker.'

Ronnie smiled, 'Yes Mum, can you hear me?'

'Oh yes, loud and clear although you sound like you're in a tunnel.'

'That sounds about right,' said Ronnie, tracing the pentacle with her fingertips. 'It's good to hear your voice Mum.'

'Now I'm hands free I can shuffle…tell me when to stop and how many to pick.'

Ronnie allowed a few seconds to go by, opening her mind to the great Goddess and spirits of nature and knowing her mother would be doing the same.

Minerva didn't have time to light a candle but she envisioned it, just like the circle of protection she was casting in her mind. A good Witch was an imaginative one. And from all her years of experience with the cards, she knew how life often presented the need for a reading without always the time to prepare for it.

'Stop,' said Ronnie, 'and three from the top.'

As Minerva stopped shuffling and picked three cards, she realized a fourth card sticking to the others. 'There's four here, so we'll call that our first piece of guidance shall we?'

'Whatever you say Mum. What is it?'

Minerva straightened up in the small bed and looked across at Isis, still sleeping quite soundly. 'For a start, four is the number of stability, firm foundations and order. So I'd say you are needing this at the moment, while...' her voice trailed off and back again, 'the Ten of Cups, being that fourth card, says a happy family will provide you with that. Which means that it's not the material things but the *quality* of relationships within your family unit which gives you the ultimate security, does that make sense?'

Her mother and the cards always made sense, in fact she couldn't remember a time when they didn't. 'It does, yes, go on...'

'And then, right next to that we have the Four of Pentacles which is talking about not wanting to let go of something, usually something physical, like money. But it comes from some kind of possessiveness and *that* is always rooted in a fear of change.'

Ronnie banged her boots against the straw bale. 'Could that involve a person?'

'Yes it could,' Minerva replied. 'Especially if you have someone like the Emperor next to it, implying a bossy sort of bloke, dominant perhaps. I'd say jealousy could be coming up, but anyway, let's move on...and we finish with the Nine of Pentacles. Well I never!'

'And what's that?' pressed Ronnie, biting her lip. Her mother always went off in a world of her own as if the cards were coming to life right in front of her. And as far as Minerva was concerned, they were. The tarot was a living thing.

'This is the ultimate kind of self-reliance, often reflected in self employment of some kind. So to summarize, we have a situation where there are all the ingredients for security- plenty of money opportunities – but there's a problem with someone who's trying for some reason, to stop that from happening, who may not be aware that's what they're doing, but it's only because they're feeling insecure when all they want in the world is to be part of a happy family...which means more than anything else.'

She stopped while Ronnie sat in stunned silence. 'Mum, can you pick another card please?'

She waited while Minerva went to work again. 'Queen of Swords. A need to make a decision without your emotions getting in the way. It's time to face the truth.'

Ronnie was quiet. There was always so much information and Minerva always gave the meanings quite impartially to start with, leaving it up to the recipient to interpret their own meaning in the cards.

But Ronnie wasn't sure. She could make out all the cards but one...the Emperor. Could it be her or Allan Key? She didn't feel like she was being overpowering and dominant at the moment but she could see how he might be doing that on the most subtle of levels with Joe. And Joe being band blind was going along for the ride, and why not? She couldn't blame him, at all. It was like being offered a super size carrot, dangling by the drumstick of Allan Key.

She could see herself in the Four of Pentacles, not wanting to let go of Joe because she wanted them to be a happy family and how could that be if he went away? What was she frightened of? Losing Joe? Losing anyone would be more like it. But also, that same card could apply to Allan Key too. Maybe he wanted to hang onto the band as it might be the happy family he'd never had.

'Any questions?'

Her mother's voice trickled over the phone and she swallowed hard for a moment, rearranging the straw pentacle.

'Only one, how do you know who to trust?'

Ronnie heard her mother's sigh and waited for the answer. 'Let's pick another one shall we? There's always room for one more card!'

Ronnie waited on the other end as her mother shuffled once more.

'Well, well, well!' said Minerva at last.

'What is it Mum?'

'The World, which in relation to your question is perfect. The one to trust here is *the universe,* because this is success and celebration on every level. Trusting in life itself is the only thing which will truly bring you fulfillment.'

Ronnie groaned, 'Oh Mum!'

'It's wonderful darling isn't it? Success, right here and now!'

'No Mum it's not, because I'm not sure how to do that! If I knew all that I wouldn't have asked for guidance would I? How is that supposed to help me?'

There was a moment of quiet before Minerva started talking again, this time in much softer tones. 'Ronnie, you need to stop doubting yourself. Now I know that sounds simplistic but it doesn't mean it's any less useful. You have all the answers, you just need to trust yourself.'

'But that's just it, I don't at the moment!'

'Ron, stop for one minute and think. At the very worst times of your life so far, hasn't everything worked out? Hasn't life come up trumps for you? Look what you have, a beautiful daughter, a loving partner, a lovely place to live, the animals – your life itself is idyllic in so many ways!'

Ronnie sighed. 'Yeah, I know what you're saying, but sometimes I just can't seem to see it like that!'

'That's only because you're allowing your emotions to get in the way. Time to hang out with the Queen of Swords, she'll soon sort you out.'

Minerva looked across the room at Isis beginning to stir under the covers. 'Ronnie darling, whatever it is, it's not worth worrying about, believe me.'

Ronnie stuck a piece of straw into her mouth and began to chew. 'Easy for *you* to say Mum. Anyway thanks, good to know everything's going to work out in the end.'

'Doesn't it always darling?'

Minerva felt the first signs of a hot flush and remembered the impending taxidermist's visit. Leaping out of the room and into the coolness of the corridors she made her way past various dead animals to the landing.

Face to face with the three-legged black sheep, she sighed into the handset. 'Look Ron, have a little faith in yourself and just remember there are always those who are worse off than you. Sometimes when all else fails it's the only way to think.'

Ronnie thought of Gavin and his Mum and smiled weakly at the straw pentacle, 'I know, you're right Mum. Thanks for that anyway. How are things going your end?'

'Well, we have a dead parrot on our hands already, would you believe?'

'Not Roger?'

'The very one, I'm afraid, gone to the great perch in the sky. But it's okay because the taxidermist is coming today to put things right.'

'You mean stuff him?'

'By the very man, Mr. I. Stuffham himself. He's German you know, and good at his job if the evidence round here is anything to go by. There are stuffed animals everywhere.'

Ronnie watched as a rat scuttled from under the pallets of

straw bales and across the tack room floor. Lifting her feet up high she screeched down the phone, 'At least you know they're dead!'

'Of course they're dead,' said Minerva, glancing up at a scrawny looking chicken with one eye, 'The idea of a mass resurrection doesn't bear thinking about, in *this* of all places, Ron. It's not your average five star hotel I can assure you.'

She wrinkled her nose at the musty odour hanging about the landing.

'Come on Mum, it's Aunt Crow's place we're talking about here...surely you weren't expecting any different?'

Minerva felt a cold shiver run down her back and tightened her dressing gown, 'I'm not sure what I expected to be honest, but I can tell you Spellstead Hall is a law unto itself and definitely *not* for the faint-hearted.'

Just at that moment, there was a scream from the end of the hallway.

'Must go, Ronnie darling,' said Minerva hurrying back to the bedroom, 'I think Didge the snake could be making another appearance. Isis may not be appreciating the wake up call.'

Ronnie smiled to herself. No, a snake wasn't the most appealing of sleeping partners, but at least her mother and Isis had each other for company, and battling the odds together, they'd come back stronger.

She was sure of it.

17

The Great Escape

Breakfast at Spellstead wasn't conventional by any means. The uninitiated could be forgiven for all kinds of reactive behaviour to the strangest of causes, as was the case with Minerva and Isis and their assortment of dining companions, day or night, both inside and outside the house.

One very cold day, two of these four-legged diners were waiting for their breakfast at the gate of the small paddock beside the overgrown vegetable garden.

'I've never been up close to a llama before, have you Isis?' said Minerva, boldly striding ahead with arms full of hay.

Still shaky from her early morning visitor, Isis took a while to answer. 'I haven't, no. What are their names?'

'Spit and Polish would you believe? Can't for the life of me think why Aunt Crow would call them that. Ridiculous if you ask me. Nothing magical in those names at all!'

Isis couldn't think straight, let alone walk straight and was keeping as close to Minerva as she could as the biting wind whipped around them. When Minerva stopped abruptly at the gate, Isis didn't; slamming into her as a brutal gust of wind blew the hood from her poncho over her face. This pushed Minerva against the gate with such force and at such close quarters to the two shaggy coated creatures, it took her breath away.

'Oh my Goddess!' cried Minerva as one of the llamas spat something at her face.

It wouldn't have been so bad if it was only Minerva the stinking globules of slime landed on, but as Isis was directly behind her, she was hit too. 'Oh my god!' screamed Isis, immediately regretting opening her mouth as the slime caught her bottom lip and slipped inside. Minerva's face was so contorted it was no wonder she couldn't speak, repulsion can be very dis-figuring.

Isis however, screamed like a banshee, spitting out as much as she could as fast as she could. 'Yuck, yuck, YUCK!'

While Isis doubled over trying to rid herself of every bit of the nasty substance, Minerva stood frozen, hand over her mouth and eyes shut. 'I take it that was Spit, the vile bastard!' she said finally, glaring at the culprit who was casually chewing hay.

'It was spit all right,' wailed Isis. 'I've never tasted anything so foul!'

At this point the other llama leaned over the gate and began to frantically lick Minerva's face in a circular motion.

'Oh my Goddess,' cried Minerva, unable to move 'What's it doing?!'

'I think that's Polish!' screamed Isis above the wind.

Oblivious to the havoc he had caused, Spit continued to chew hay as Polish licked every exposed piece of flesh he could find, while Minerva, eyes and mouth shut tight, remained catatonic throughout.

Meanwhile, Isis stood behind Minerva, taking full advantage of her human shield. But so close an encounter was bound to have its drawbacks and before Isis had a chance to recoil from the advances of Polish, his enormous tongue was slurping up and down and round until her cheeks glistened with spittle.

Unfortunately, the pitiful cries of the two women were deafened by the elements as they fought bravely against wind and slime. Not even the nature spirits could hear them.

'Is Spit still there?' screeched Minerva, still fastened against the gate with her eyes shut.

'He's eating', murmured a glistening Isis, pinned against Minerva.

'Do you have any wet wipes on you?'

'No,' came the muffled reply.

Minerva made a great effort to move, pushing Isis so hard she bent over like a pipe cleaner, falling onto the muddy path. This gave Minerva the room to move away from the gate, toppling over Isis and the crumpled orange poncho and diving head first onto the mud.

'Argh!' cried Minerva, with a mouthful of hay as well as slime, 'What are you *doing* Isis?!'

'You're crushing me!' The pitiful reply was carried away by the roar of the wind as both parties struggled to find their feet and grabbing each other, scrambled up to a standing position.

Coughing and spluttering like two battle worn soldiers they stumbled back in the direction of Spellstead Hall. The wind was now behind them, shooing them along the hay strewn, muddy path until they were a safe enough distance away from the enemy to stop for a moment.

Minerva turned to Isis. 'Come to think about it, I did wonder why Aunt Crow didn't mention those foul creatures until she was leaving, did you notice that?'

Isis pushed the poncho hood back to reveal shining, beetroot cheeks. 'I didn't realize there were so many strange animals to look after. It's a challenge isn't it?'

'A *challenge?*' snorted Minerva, 'It's a nightmare. I'm not going anywhere near those two little humpless camels again, they can damn well starve for all I care!' Grabbing the corners of the orange poncho, she wiped her face roughly, removing every last trace of slime.

'We can't do that Minerva, I'm sure we can work out a way of throwing the hay in without coming into contact with them.'

'Ah, but they're devious blighters aren't they? One false move and before you know it there's a gob of rotten slime perfectly aimed and fired. I had no idea such disgusting bodily fluids existed!'

'Well they *are* animals!'

'I wouldn't subject my worst enemy to anything as grim as that.'

Minerva stopped, clutching her throat and retched while Isis looked on in bewilderment, patting her back. 'We've just got to get on with it. Worse things have happened at sea.'

Minerva continued to cough and splutter out any lingering and slimy remains.

'Are you all right?' said Isis.

Minerva pulled herself up, still clutching onto the poncho, 'Do I look all right? After the slime attack from hell is it any wonder? What's that over there?'

She pointed weakly at the drive leading up to the house. It was a long and winding unmade road disappearing and reappearing over the humps and bumps of the surrounding landscape. And creeping up towards them was a dark shape and the sound of an engine.

Isis screwed her eyes up in the direction of Minerva's finger. 'Is it someone on a motorbike? I can hear an engine.'

Minerva peered into the distance. 'You're right Isis, it *is* a motorbike. I've no idea who it could be, we haven't seen anyone for days.'

'Are we expecting anyone?' said Isis, feeling for her hairpiece.

'The taxidermist is *supposed* to be coming at some point. You never know, Steve McQueen might have decided to pay us a visit.'

'I thought he was dead.'

Minerva sighed. 'Of course he's dead. He snuffed it years ago, but don't you remember the film, The Great Escape?'

They watched as the bike ascended the hill, and saw as it rumbled into view that it wasn't just a motorbike but a motorbike with a sidecar attached to it. Grinding to a wobbly halt in front of them, a small hunched figure sat up and dismounted awkwardly.

Minerva whispered under her breath, 'Hardly Steve McQueen is it?'

She stared at the little man as he removed his goggles and helmet, a thick thatch of snow white hair springing out beneath it. 'There's the great escape…right under his hat.'

The man tucked his helmet and goggles under one arm and standing to attention, ran his hand through the thick white hair, revealing the bluest pair of eyes Minerva had ever seen. 'Is it a werewolf do you think?'

Isis tutted loud enough for Minerva to hear and hoped the wolf man hadn't. Two piercing blue eyes peered out from beneath his snowy fringe but still he didn't say a word.

'Can we help you at all? Are you looking for anything or

anyone in particular?' said Minerva, drawing herself up to full height.

'I am Ivan Stuffham.'

The German accent cut through the wind as it hurled around them and Minerva brightened, 'Of course, the taxidermist!'

'Indeed,' came the curt reply. 'And you are Lady Crow's niece is that right?'

Isis turned to Minerva. 'Lady Crow?'

'It's what he calls her,' hissed Minerva. 'Yes, I am her niece, Minerva Crafty.' She shot her arm out towards him and they shook hands. It seemed like the right thing to do under the circumstances and Minerva felt a shock of electricity run up her arm and round her body. 'We've been expecting you, Mr. Stuffham.'

'So, I am here,' said the wolf man with quiet confidence. 'This is an inconvenience?'

'Not at all,' replied Minerva. 'We've finished our chores for now. Would you like a coffee before you start? Or I can do you a brandy schnapps if you'd prefer?'

The bright blue eyes sparkled. 'That will be most acceptable. I shall bring my equipment in, and if you can show me the specimen, I will make the necessary preparations.'

Isis turned to Minerva, looking worried. 'Hadn't we ought to give him a proper send off first, Minerva?'

'He's only just got here, Isis!'

'I'm talking about Roger, not Mr.—'

'—Stoofham,' said the wolf man bending over and delving into the sidecar, 'at your service ladies!'

He hauled out a brown leather holdall far bigger than he was and began to walk towards Spellstead Hall with great purpose into the prevailing wind. The two friends exchanged a bemused look and without saying a word, followed him.

'We can drum Roger over the hedge once he's been prepared,' said Minerva. 'It'll be much better that way, Isis, you'll see.'

'I'll take your word for it,' said Isis. 'The stuffing man seems to know what he's doing, so perhaps you're right.'

Minerva spun around. 'I *know* I'm right, Isis. And to be quite honest, it'll be a relief to let someone else take the reins in this situation.'

'I know, we haven't been doing too well in the animal husbandry department so far have we?'

'But we're still here, even if Roger isn't and there's only one thing to do, Isis, and that's make the best of it. And after the kind of start we've had today, I'd say a brandy schnapps breakfast is a grand idea.'

Isis caught the scent of dried llama slime and wrinkled her nose. 'It looks like it, yes,' she said, pulling her poncho around her and walking on ahead.

Minerva followed with renewed confidence and a bounce in her stride. Things were looking up at last.

* * *

Ivan Stuffham knocked back the last dregs of his schnapps. 'I will get to work now,' he said, standing up and reaching for his bag.

Minerva noticed how much the brandy had gone down in the short time they had spent in the kitchen. She for one, was feeling a lot less stressed now after the llama episode and if the semi-horizontal person beside her was anything to go by, so was Isis. Slumped across the kitchen table beneath her poncho, Isis reminded her of a bat.

'Is there anything you need?' Minerva called out to the upright and perfectly balanced figure as he marched slowly out of the kitchen.

'No,' came the curt reply, 'I have everything in here, thank you.'

Minerva watched as the bag and Ivan Stuffham side-stepped a grunting Brenda, making it through the doorway and out into the dimly lit hall. She couldn't help but wonder how he was going to work in such dark conditions and after propping up Isis with a bag of flour, she followed him.

Bent over the gaping sides of the canvas bag, the snowy haired German worked quickly to lift out a metal frame which sprang into a fold down table onto which he placed a wireless lamp. Suddenly, the area transformed into a pool of light and Minerva was intrigued, edging towards the brightly lit operating table like a moth to a flame. She wasn't going to miss the chance of seeing this stage of the process in action if she could help it.

'Do you mind if I watch?'

'Not at all.'

'I'm fascinated to see what happens!'

Mr. Stuffham didn't reply. He was too busy arranging his operátus while Minerva stood behind him. She watched in silence as he drew out of the bag a folded piece of cloth and opened it out one fold at a time. Removing a handful of metal, he laid out the scalpels carefully on the table under the spotlight. He arranged his tools in silence, peering out from beneath a white shock of hair when he was finished. 'Where is the specimen?'

'Oh yes,' said Minerva, 'I'd almost forgotten.'

The bright blue eyes flashed at her.

'I'll just get him,' she called softly behind her as she padded up the hallway in the direction of the utility room.

Cradling the cold plastic bag, Minerva retraced her steps and placed Roger on the operating table. Mr Stuffham looked up through the snowy curtains of his fringe and muttered under his breath, 'I cannot work on the specimen in this condition.'

Minerva narrowed her eyes, flitting them back and forth between Roger and the German. 'What do you mean?'

'He is too cold.'

'Well yes, he's dead,' said Minerva, the first seeds of doubt niggling inside her. She flinched as the piercing eyes fixed themselves on her, 'Oh yes of course, I see what you mean.'

She turned the frozen and feathered form over on the table, wishing with all her might for the thing to thaw out right there. 'How long will it take?' she said, not taking her eyes off Roger.

'Some hours for sure,' said Mr. Stuffham, running a hand through the snowy thatch of hair to reveal a flat, square-shaped forehead.

Minerva took a slow step back. This was not how it was supposed to go. What if this strange little man wasn't actually a man at all? What if he was half man and half monster? What was she going to do with him?

'Right,' said Minerva, feeling far from it, 'Will you be able to wait until he thaws out or will you go and come back?'

She realized she didn't have a clue how far away he lived.

'Do you have more brandy?'

'There's always more brandy…schnapps?'

He nodded. 'It will help to pass the time.'

Minerva wondered if putting Roger in the microwave would help to pass the time quicker but thought better of it and led the way back to the kitchen where Isis lay slumped and snoozing while Brenda hoovered up around her.

Grabbing the brandy bottle and two clean glasses she signalled to the taxidermist to sit down. 'Cheers,' she said, raising her glass, and concentrating all her thoughts into a ball of light, she sent it to Roger and his insides. With a bit of magic, it would reach him before the brandy numbed out the insides of the snowy haired German.

She wanted this over and done with.

* * *

Isis opened one eye and found herself staring into an empty brandy bottle. The distant murmuring of voices in the hallway was getting louder. It sounded like singing, a lot like singing in fact. Wasn't that the German national anthem? Her father had been in a brass band for years with a German conductor who always made them play that particular piece in every performance. She knew it off by heart.

When a fuzzy form appeared in the kitchen doorway she pushed herself up onto her elbows and blinked until the figure came into full focus. 'Is that you Minerva?'

The faraway reply came eventually, 'Did you think I was Gerald?'

At the mention of his name, Isis sat upright and blinked again. He was part of another lifetime, a lifetime so far removed from where she was she wondered if she'd dreamed him up. 'No, I didn't think you were Gerald. I'm not *stupid* Minerva, I can see perfectly clearly.'

Minerva chuckled. 'You mean you've sobered up. Well I'm glad to hear that at least one of us has, well two of us actually…' she smoothed down the thick folds of her green chenille jumper and brushed off some loose strands of hay, 'which is more than can be said for Mr Stuffing out there.'

She turned her head in the direction of the German national anthem and winced.

Isis yawned and stretched out her arms and feet, almost slipping off her chair in the process. 'You mean Steve McQueen's still here? I thought he would take Roger away.'

Minerva crossed her arms and leaned against the door frame. 'Oh no, he's much too interested in the brandy schnapps. He's on his second bottle now. It wasn't helped by the fact that Roger was frozen, so waiting for the great thaw has been a bit of a trial. The German national anthem is now imprinted on my brain forever.'

'Oh poor Roger! Will he survive do you think?'

Minerva wrinkled her brows. 'Isis, in case you hadn't noticed, the parrot is dead!'

'Yes I know but he should still be treated properly – I mean with respect – surely?'

'He *is* being treated properly,' snapped Minerva, uncrossing her arms. 'He's being stuffed like all the others round here.'

'Yes, but the stuffing man is drunk, you say.'

Minerva placed her hands on her hips. 'Well that can't be helped I'm afraid. What was I supposed to give him, tea and toast?'

'It would have kept him sober.'

'I really don't think it'll be a problem Isis, trust me. For all his *strangeness*, he's a professional. Aunt Crow wouldn't employ someone who didn't know what they were doing!'

'But not when they're drunk!'

'Look, he'll be fine, everything's fine. Will you stop fretting about every little thing!'

'I hope you're right.'

'Of course I'm right. Roger will look himself again in no time, and carefully placed back on his perch, no-one will know any different, you'll see.'

'Not even Aunt Crow? He *was* her favourite pet and he wasn't the quietest creature.'

'The foulest thing on this earth you mean, it's not such a bad thing he's gone.'

'I can't believe you said that!'

'Well I just did and if you can just climb down off that high horse of yours, we can move on with this whole messy affair. Aunt Crow will be back soon and I don't want her upset.'

'But she will be when she finds out...'

'No she won't, because I have some magic up my sleeve which will sort that minor problem out, just you wait. It never fails.'

Isis couldn't think straight. All she wanted was Gerald. Gerald and his strong brown arms and golden smile. Gerald with his reassuring squeezes and earthy scent which *did* things to her. She didn't want to face Aunt Crow and her grief and she didn't want to know what magic Minerva was conjuring up to deal with it, whatever it was.

She wanted to go home.

18

Goddess Talk

Ronnie stared into the bottom of her mug before downing the last dregs of cold tea. The ticking of the clock on the wall weaved its hypnotic spell, startling her when it struck twelve harsh chords. Joe would be back soon, band rehearsals didn't normally go on this long. He was always back before midnight.

But that was before Allan Key arrived on the scene.

She didn't like it and thought about what the tarot had said, smiling as her mother's voice came into her head, *'You're all at sixes and sevens darling...but don't worry, it'll pass. Everything does in the end.'*

'She's right, you know.'

Looking over at the old armchair in the corner she wasn't at all surprised to see the boat's previous owner sitting comfortably, as if he'd been there forever, with the white cat on his lap.

'Is she?' said Ronnie, quite calmly, 'You'd know I suppose, Ropey.'

The old man chuckled and turned to look at her. 'Just

because I'm dead doesn't mean to say I know it all but I do have a pretty good idea about life now that I'm gone. Funny that'.

'But you're not gone. Are you here all the time?' asked Ronnie, wondering how much he knew about their lives.

'When I think about the old girl, somehow I find myself here, yes. It's hard to be anywhere else really but I can tell you this, young lady, she'll look after you, will Freya. She's not just a boat.'

Ronnie thought of the great warrior woman in the chariot out on the deck and felt a familiar twinge. 'Funny you should say that,' she said slowly, 'I do feel a presence about the place.'

Ropey nodded. 'Does she speak to you?'

'Well, now you mention it…'

'I thought so,' said Ropey, grinning. 'If you have the gift she'll find a way of getting through to you. Plain as day, she'd speak to me just like I'm talking to you now…showing up just when I needed her, always with a timely piece of advice and I was grateful for that. She looked after us didn't she girl?'

He bent over the fluffy white creature on his lap and fell quiet as Ronnie strained her eyes at the ghostly pair. 'Will she hear me if I call her?'

All she could see was Ropey's toothless grin and raised hand as he faded away. When he was gone completely she walked across to the chair, where a large tuft of white hair lay on the threadbare arm, and touched the indent on the seat.

It was warm.

A current of energy surged up her spine and she rushed out to the front deck, where the stillness of midnight hung over the gently swilling water, and stopped in front of the painted Goddess. Freya in all her glory was brimming with a strange glow, the fading paintwork radiating a life of its own.

What if she was a person like Ronnie was?

She knew it wasn't just a painting, but a portal to another world. And the voice when it came did not surprise her.

'Hail Rhiannon! Your mother named you well and she was right, you are growing into its magic, for words are power and in that name is *your* power. Nothing is more sacred to your being than the name you were given at birth.'

Ronnie looked up at Freya and felt the surge of energy inside her growing, making her bigger somehow. 'Well, I'm glad you think so,' she said to the Goddess, 'because I'm not really feeling it at the moment if I'm honest. In fact, I feel quite powerless!'

The Goddess laughed and shimmered on the wall in front of her. 'Perhaps some guidance will not go amiss, that's why I'm here.'

'What do I need to know?'

Ronnie surprised herself with her directness, but wanted to make the most of the opportunity while it was there. It wasn't every day she got to speak to a Goddess.

'There are earthly guides and there are magical ones, all will appear at the right time. Your sacred animal, the horse, is your magical guide on this earthly plane and you know this. Your old friend has shown himself to you and will continue to do so but do not ignore your new friend in this earthly realm. He has just as much to give in ways you are not aware of right now.'

'You mean Lazarus? He's a strong little fella that's for sure,' pondered Ronnie, 'And he's certainly helped me to get over losing Bob. Morrigan loves him too, so does Crow Bird…'

'And there it is,' said Freya. 'His name means the helper of all who come into contact with him. This works in many ways, for he who has received divine assistance in turn touches the lives of those around him.'

'A bit like an enlightened being? Is that what you're saying?'

Ronnie glanced quickly around in the moonlight, checking to see if there was anyone else around. Thankfully she was alone. It wasn't every day one spotted a barmy young woman having a conversation with a painting on a boat at midnight.

'Enlightenment is neither found in another or given by the selective few. It comes from within. Yes, there are some who appear to be the chosen ones but all souls have the capacity to grow from the inside out. It is the birthright of each individual. Every soul chooses his path and walks it, according to the laws of the magical realms. It is the way of things.'

'Even animals?' said Ronnie. 'How can they know these things without the so called intelligence that we humans have?'

As soon as she said it she thought of Bob and the connection between them. She thought of how he knew her every thought and feeling and she thought of all the times he'd shown up lately.

'Yes you are right in your assumption that in between the worlds there are no barriers when it comes to soul connections. Death does not separate those who have great love for each other.'

Ronnie could feel a tightening in her throat and hot tears pricking her eyes. 'Animals feel it too, I know that' she whispered. 'My relationship with Bob was special and will always be special because—'

'—He still lives,' said the Goddess, 'and bound by the ties of the purest form, he is in truth, closer than you think. It is not difficult to understand when you are able to see past illusion, when the fog has lifted and the soul is touched enough to wake up to its true purpose.'

Ronnie frowned and couldn't take it all in. Freya's words seemed to take on a life of their own, sweeping through her mind in a huge vacuum, clearing out every doubt.

Freya laughed softly. 'Small doses of magical wisdom are best at first. You need time to digest these simple but great truths and turn them over to your higher self, the soul essence. Do not try too hard young maiden! The sword and the shield are your tools to cut away old patterns of thinking, to carve out a new path and protect you from the enemy of past grievances and those who would darken your light. Do not let them. Hold up your head and heart and honour who you are. Hail Rhiannon!'

And she was gone.

The painting was no longer alive and talking but had faded in the moonlight to a dull hue Ronnie could hardly see. She stood staring at it, stunned into silence.

Am I going mad? she thought, as the sound of a vehicle rumbled down the marina drive towards the boat. The shadow cast by the van pulling up, the low, mumbling voices, the slamming of a door, all teetered on the edge of her awareness somewhere in the far distance.

She tried to stay where she was and ignore the sounds but before she knew it a warm kiss planted itself on her cold cheek. 'What the hell are you doing out here Ron? Been howling under that moon?' Joe's breath was warm and he stank of weed.

As the vehicle rumbled off in the distance, she turned to see him standing there in the moonlight with his guitar case in one hand. She tried to gather her thoughts but all she could think about was how stunning he looked in the moonlight. A hazy glow of silver outlined his head, his wavy hair glinting a celestial hue. 'You look like an angel.'

He laughed. 'Maybe that's because I am.'

'Maybe you're right.'

Their words hung in the air like stars as the moon continued to beam across their faces. All the earlier friction between them had gone.

'And you, my lady,' he said, putting his guitar down and drawing her into his arms, 'are a Goddess in the flesh. So that makes us pretty well suited wouldn't you say?'

'I'd say you've got a way to go before you reach Godly status,' smiled Ronnie. 'Until then, watch your step, it's a long way down.'

'Oh no,' laughed Joe, 'Not a fallen angel! I might just have to drag you down with me, don't count on me going down quietly.'

He nudged her towards the French doors and they laughed together as Joe stopped by Freya, 'You know what? I could swear she's in on it too.'

'What do you mean?' said Ronnie, studying his face.

'Those eyes, they follow you around wherever you go, haven't you noticed? She's alive, I swear she is. It's as if she knows our every move.'

Ronnie didn't say a word, but glanced quickly at Freya as she followed Joe through the doors. The paintwork glowed in the moonlight and the eyes of the Goddess caught her own just for a second as the corners of her mouth turned up at the edges. It was so subtle no one else would have noticed.

But Ronnie did.

* * *

Minerva was up before sunrise on the day of Aunt Crow's return. There was a lot to do and not a minute to waste if she was to fit it all in before her aunt walked back through the doors of Spellstead Hall. She must do her utmost magical best to prepare and gather the ingredients needed before the sun was fully up. The spell would begin to lose its power otherwise.

'Now then,' she said to herself, chewing the end of her pen, 'I need some red ochre ink, where the *hell* am I going to get hold of that?'

Her eyes flitted around the hallway and up the winding stairs and following her instincts, she passed the dusty cases of dead animals until she reached the bedroom. Pushing the door back slowly only made it creak louder and Isis shot up like a jack-in-a-box in the far corner.

'What? Who's that? Gerald is that you?' she screeched, her hairpiece toppling dangerously over one shoulder.

'No! It's me,' hissed Minerva. 'Isis, do you have any of that red ink with you? You know, that stuff which you paint on your skin?'

'You mean henna?' said Isis, rubbing her eyes.

'Oh is that what it is?' said Minerva, 'It'll have to do I suppose. It really should be ochre but as long as it's the colour of *blood*, that's the main thing.'

Isis was already scrambling around in her bag and eventually pulled out a small box. 'What do you want it for and why are you up so early?'

'Magic is of course the answer to both questions,' said Minerva, '*Interview with a Corpse* spell to be precise. It's the perfect way to tie up this messy business with Roger and it needs to be done by sunrise.'

Isis looked baffled. 'And what does it entail?'

'It's not about the tail of anything, but Roger's beak, actually,' said Minerva, checking the crumpled piece of paper in her hand. '*Write on an evergreen leaf in ochre or better still, menstrual blood...* which of course is completely out of the question.'

Isis looked horrified. 'Speak for yourself.'

Minerva narrowed her eyes at Isis. 'In which case, can you oblige?'

'No,' said a beetroot faced Isis, 'No I can't. I've two weeks to go before...'

'Oh all right, you're in the clear then,' said Minerva. 'Thank the Goddess we don't have to tackle that particular ingredient, but the next best thing—' she pondered over the box of inks, '—will have to be this I suppose. And now you're up, I'd appreciate a hand with it. It's a delicate matter and may not be easy to perform.'

'Perform?' said Isis, pulling her poncho over her head and rescuing her dangling hairpiece.

'Isis,' said Minerva, staring hard at the wall in front of her, 'this is not the time for a thousand questions, I'll explain as we go. Now can you please get a move on and follow me.'

In a flurry of turquoise and orange, Isis pulled on her sandals, and feeling a twinge of excitement she scurried after the frantic Minerva. Grabbing Roger's cage and a spade from outside, Minerva called behind her as she marched towards the llama paddock, 'Isis, the brandy! We'll be needing it for the libations.'

Isis made a quick detour to the kitchen, managing to clear with inches to spare, a snoring and bloated looking Brenda and a sleeping Didge. Grabbing the brandy and holding her breath, she launched herself back over the unlikely pair and fled out of the kitchen and into the darkest hour before the dawn.

* * *

Bending over a freshly dug hole wasn't the best of conditions for magic as far as Minerva was concerned, but it would have to do. She liked to think the more challenges one was presented with, the more satisfying the reward. And usually, that meant the more effective the result would be.

Isis held onto Roger's cage and glanced nervously across the landscape of rolling hills, noticing a faint red glow in the distance. 'The sun's not far off, Minerva,' she mumbled, chewing the corners of her mouth.

Minerva stopped digging. 'Not far off? Don't be ridiculous, Isis, it's millions of miles away.'

Isis sighed. 'You know what I mean, Minerva. It's coming up and I thought this had to be done before that happened, not *while* it was happening?'

'Yes, well I'm going as fast as I can, Isis, the deed is almost done.'

Minerva sighed heavily as she leaned against the spade for a moment, surveying her handiwork. The hole was hardly a ditch but it was big enough to accommodate the two of them plus Roger which was all they needed. She made one last attempt to make the space larger by scraping away at the sides with as much force as she could muster, and then threw the spade down with a flourish. 'That will have to do,' she said, stepping down into the muddy hole and signalling for Isis to join her. 'Can you manage?'

'You want me to get in as well?'

'That's the general idea, yes,' said Minerva, 'And as you so kindly reminded me, there's no time to lose.'

She tutted loudly and removed from her cloak a bulging

satchel and began to open and spread its contents before her on the ledge: A clump of bay leaves and fennel plus the box of henna ink and a large twig she'd picked up off the ground on the way there.

Isis peered into the large hole in the ground. 'Do I have to?'

Minerva scanned the ingredients. 'The brandy, Isis, do you have it?'

Isis put the cage down, fumbling beneath her poncho and handed Minerva a half full bottle of brandy. Glancing into the cage, Isis hesitated. 'He doesn't look any different, are you sure he's…'

'Stuffed? Oh yes, I made sure of that,' snapped Minerva. 'I watched the old boy like a hawk for the rest of the operation. It took him long enough and half a bottle of this stuff into the bargain, but there, it's done now. And you're absolutely right, Isis, you wouldn't know would you? He looks just the same as he always did. Aunt Crow won't know any difference either. And after we've finished here, he'll be as good as new.'

Isis watched as Minerva removed a jar of myrrh from the satchel and placed it into a dish, lighting a small piece of charcoal beside it. While she waited for the charcoal to burn through, she took the henna from the box and with the broken twig began to write on a large laurel leave very meticulously.

When she finished, Isis handed the cage over and Minerva attempted to place the leaf into Roger's beak. 'Oh come on,' she whispered loudly, 'I really don't want to force the issue!'

Isis looked on in horror. 'Minerva, what are you doing?'

'Binding the spell, Isis. By placing words into the mouth of the corpse, things are set into motion. Once this tricky bit is done the magic is activated, and by summoning the *Keepers* from the hidden realms to assist us, all will be well. Putting words into the mouth of the deceased will give him the power of speech once more, or at least Aunt Crow will believe that's the case which amounts to the same thing.'

'Oh, I see,' said Isis, looking bewildered.

She knew better than to keep asking questions at a time like this. Minerva needed every bit of concentration, leaving plenty of time to go through the finer details when it was over, which if the sun's position was anything to go by, would be soon.

By the time Minerva had managed to secure the laurel leaf inside Roger's beak, she carefully placed him back in the cage, shutting the door behind him. Propping it up on the inside of the ditch she surrounded the cage with the burning myrrh and sprigs of wormwood. Taking the brandy, she removed the lid and poured the smallest amount around the cage, carefully reciting her chosen words:

'Hecate, come! from worlds between,
Nothing like we've ever seen,
Nothing like we've ever known,
Come plant with us and seeds be sown!
Turn the tide around again
Reverse the grief, remove the pain,
Roger as he was before and Aunt Crow never asking more.
All is bound and now complete,
Success upon this magical feat!
By power of Land and Sky and Sea
As I will, so mote it be!'

A still and eerie silence hung in the cold morning air as if Hecate herself was there among them, gracing the dark earth with her presence. Even the llamas stood motionless by the paddock gate, their long necks craning together like a pair of question marks.

Minerva stared into the distance and down again at the cage while Isis held her breath and forced herself to keep still. It was a tense and magical moment. 'I don't suppose you have anything on you that you could *bang* have you, Isis?'

'Bang? You mean like a drum?'

Minerva rolled her eyes. 'Yes, like a drum. I didn't bring mine.'

'Shall I go and get a couple of saucepans and wooden spoons?'

'Oh no, you can't do that,' barked Minerva, 'Not while the circle is cast. You never know what might join us if you let them... No, it's quite all right, we'll just have to clap and sing to build the energy. Are you ready?'

Isis stiffened inside her poncho and nodded obediently while Minerva clapped enthusiastically and chanted the words of the spell over again. Watching Minerva's lips carefully as she chanted, Isis followed her lead. And before long, the words, although stilted and hesitant at first, began to take on an energy of their own, rising and falling with each breath and threading themselves together in a web of power.

The llamas stood transfixed and staring at the two humans who seemed oblivious to anything except for the crudely dug hole they swayed around in. Bending one way and then the other, Minerva and Isis wobbled out of time until eventually, like two pendulums, they fell into a rhythm and became one.

As the sun climbed slowly in the sky, Isis completely forgot where she was just as Minerva remembered who was coming home later. It was going to be an interesting day, she thought, as she gazed into the cage. But first she must look for the super glue and fix Roger back on his perch.

If her memory served her right, there was nothing wrong with Aunt Crow's eyesight.

19

Secrets and Sorcery

Ronnie buried her face in the tufts of coarse mane and ran her hands over a bony shoulder blade. 'You're still a bit on the skinny side, boy,' she said to Lazarus, watching his small, pointy ears flicking back and forth at the sound of her voice.

'Yeah, but thanks to you, not quite so close to death's door!'

Ronnie jumped back to see Sophia grinning at her over the stable door. 'Christ, you carry on like that and I'll be close to it myself.'

Sophia grinned. 'Come on Ron, you're tougher than that! Must be going soft in your old age.'

Ronnie shrugged and gave Lazarus a hearty pat on the rump. 'I sometimes wonder, especially at the moment.'

'Come on, out with it,' said Sophia. 'Don't tell me you're having second thoughts about your wild and watery life on the river with all those dogs and that handsome pirate of yours?'

Ronnie turned to face Sophia. 'It's Allan Key, the drummer guy. Ever since he turned up, Joe's been different. There's talk of a band tour and Joe's all excited about it and I know I shouldn't worry but I can't help it. There's something about the guy I just don't trust.'

'I know what you mean Ron, I get it. Happens to me a lot too, but you know what? There's bugger all you can do about it. If you smell a rat, you'll only make it worse by trying to prove the point and Joe won't thank you for it. Let him find out for himself if that's the case. Haven't you got enough going on with this little fella and Morrigan and all the other wonderful stuff in your life?'

Ronnie looked down at her daughter playing in the straw bed with Crow Bird and Lazarus and sighed. 'God, you're right, maybe I'm over thinking it all. But there is *one* thing though, that's only just happened...'

'Oh?' said Sophia, turning to the sound of a vehicle pulling up into the yard. 'What's that?'

Ronnie followed her gaze to the figure jumping from an old red van and heading towards them. '*That* is who I'm talking about, believe it or not.'

Sophia squinted her eyes against the watery sunshine as the figure came into focus and gasped under her breath, 'That's not who I think it is, is it?'

The sauntering gait was not unfamiliar as he approached them.

'Good-day Sophia, how's it going?' The slow drawl rolled out in a billowing mist.

'Gavin,' she said, 'What are you doing here?'

'Oh, just back for a while,' he said, glancing at Ronnie. 'Mum's not too well, so I'm here to keep an eye on her.'

'Oh I see,' said Sophia, 'I'm sorry about your mother, but it's good to see you. You're looking well!'

Gavin grinned. 'Yeah, the warmer weather makes a difference. I'd forgotten just how much colder it is over here, especially this time of year!'

He walked up to the stable door and Ronnie noticed his tanned face and closely cropped blonde hair. 'Well it *is* October!' she said, picking up her fork and tidying the straw around Lazarus.

There was an awkward silence as Gavin looked into the stable and spotted Morrigan and Crow Bird in the corner together. 'Well, well, who have we here?'

Morrigan turned her dark head around as the crow hopped onto her shoulder. It was an unusual sight and Ronnie watched Gavin's face as he grinned at her daughter. *His daughter.*

She held her breath and let it out slowly, toying with her fork. 'This is Morrigan,' she said, keeping her eyes fixed firmly on the child, 'And Crow Bird…and Lazarus.'

Her attempt to distract his attention from the child seemed to work as Gavin's eyes quickly roamed over all three of the unlikely bunch before him. His eyes lit up with amusement. 'Well, I'm very pleased to meet you and your friends, Morrigan.'

He turned to Ronnie, 'She's the spit of you isn't she? I had no idea…'

He was too busy smiling at Morrigan to see the look which passed between Sophia and Ronnie.

'Crikey, is that the time already,' said Sophia glancing at her phone, 'I have to get to work.'

'And I need to drop this young lady off at nursery,' blurted out Ronnie. 'Come on madam or we'll be late for story time!'

In a bustle of activity Ronnie hustled the toddler from the stable leaving Crow Bird talking to Lazarus as he hopped onto the pony's bony rump. Gavin chuckled at the scene and moved out of the way of mother and daughter as they piled out onto the yard. 'I take it the bird is the pony's companion too?'

'Oh yes,' said Ronnie, reaching for Morrigan's hand, 'They're all firm friends, but he stays here with the pony. It works out really well.'

'Yes, I can see that,' said Gavin, lowering his head. 'Nice to meet you Morrigan!'

For a moment, the toddler lifted her head to his and Ronnie felt a twinge of panic. 'Come on Mogs,' she said, gently tugging the child away, 'Teddy's in the car, remember? All ready for story time!'

'Teddy! Want my Teddy!'

Morrigan searched the yard for the Land Rover and began to toddle towards it, after her mother.

'I'll see you later, Sophia,' Ronnie called behind her. 'And nice to see you Gavin, take care.'

'Yeah, see you Ronnie,' said Gavin in a quiet voice, making his way to the main yard. 'Bye, bye Morrigan!'

Sophia gathered her coat and bag and followed Ronnie to where both of their vehicles were parked. 'Jesus Ron, that was a close one...' she said under her breath, searching for her car keys.

'Do you think he..?'

'I don't know, Ron. Your guess is as good as mine.'

'I suppose it had to happen sooner or later,' sighed Ronnie, lifting Morrigan into her car seat. 'I just can't think about it now Sophia, not with everything else going on...'

Sophia stopped before getting into her car. 'I wouldn't worry about it Ron, it's not worth it.'

Ronnie gave her an odd look. 'Hmm, the father of my child just turns up out of the blue and I'm supposed to take it all in my stride.'

'Yes you are.'

There was nothing else to say. Ronnie knew she was right and pecking her friend on the cheek, she stepped up into the Land Rover, smiling bravely. With a quick glance at her daughter in the back, she turned the key and caught the last of Gavin disappearing into the yard in the rear mirror. Of course she would take it all in her stride.

Gripping the steering wheel, she repeated the words over and over again until finally, the calming waves of the mantra worked its magic on her.

* * *

Back inside the kitchen at Spellstead Hall, there was a certain tension in the air as well as pig farts.

'Get that down you, Isis,' said Minerva with a peg on her nose, putting a plateful of toast and jaffa cakes next to the jar of peanut butter. 'We need to ground and prepare ourselves for what lies ahead.'

Isis, reluctant to be reminded of anything after the magic of the early morning ritual, widened her eyes in surprise. 'And what exactly is that?'

Minerva removed the peg from her nose and rubbed it hard. 'Aunt Crow, Isis, remember? She's back today…on this very morning.'

'Oh yes, I hope she's had a nice time away, it'll help to smooth things over won't it?'

Minerva frowned across the table, 'The truth is, it won't matter in the least whether she's had the holiday from hell or not.'

'Won't it?'

Minerva waved her hand to one side, reached for the brandy and poured a large shot into both of their cups. 'Of course not, she'll be well and truly spellbound. So whatever has happened or is about to happen will not affect her at all, not until it wears off, anyway. And by that time we shall be out of here, back in the land of Cragwell on Sea and in the arms of our good men.'

Isis clasped her hands together. 'Oh what a lovely thought, Minerva, I can hardly wait!'

'I must admit,' said Minerva, 'it's been a bit of a trial but we've survived haven't we?' She thought of Brenda and Didge, Spit and Polish, the countless display cases and the frozen mice in the freezer...and shivered.

'Yes, which is more than can be said for poor Roger,' said Isis, almost choking on her toast.

'These things happen I'm afraid, but at least we have done *something* to make amends. What a wonderful thing magic is, Aunt Crow won't know she's born, or more importantly, that Roger is dead!'

Chortling away at her own joke, Minerva appeared to be happy in the knowledge that all would be well.

'Wasn't it Aunt Crow who taught you all you know about magic, Minerva?'

'Indeed it was,' said Minerva, scooping out a heaped tablespoonful of peanut butter and smearing it on her toast. 'Right at the time when I needed it most. My mother was the bane of my life, stuck indoors with that Black Dog of all things. It was no wonder I gravitated towards my favourite aunt and her treehouse...and Roger,' she added in a solemn voice. 'It was the only bit of sunshine in a life of darkness. It was the only place I felt at home. One yearns for some kind of normality in the thick of everything that isn't, I can tell you.'

Isis looked around the kitchen at a grunting Brenda, now hoovering up under the table where Didge lay coiled around one of the table legs. Clamping both feet onto the rung of the chair she gazed over to the kitchen window where she could see Spit and Polish behind the smoky plumes of incense, still burning from the ceremony. Her eyes wandered back to the kitchen sink where a pile of lifeless pink, wrinkled bodies lay in a row.

'Will you give Didge his breakfast?' said Minerva casually as she began to gather up the empty plates and pile them into the sink.

Isis felt the quickening of her breath and jumped up towards the bodies on the draining board. Carefully picking one up by the end of its tail, she held it over the sleeping snake and dropped it onto the floor beside him. Not wanting to witness what happened next, she grabbed a tea-towel and began to frantically wipe up.

'We might as well have a cuppa' while we're waiting,' said Minerva, putting the kettle on. 'There's nothing else to do.'

'No, I mean yes,' mumbled Isis, making every effort not to look down. 'Sounds like a good idea…while we're waiting.'

And so they waited in companionable silence as the morning turned into the afternoon and the only sound was the freezer humming.

Isis was trying her best not to fidget. 'It's very quiet without Roger isn't it? Surely Aunt Crow will notice—'

'Isis,' said Minerva, 'Did we or did we not, work magic earlier?'

'We did.'

'And did I explain the effects of that magic to you, while you were still basking in its afterglow?'

'You did.'

'Then clearly, there is nothing to worry about!'

Isis sighed, making a valiant attempt to stop her hands from finding each other. She sat on them, swinging her legs back and forth and bit her lip so hard it hurt. 'You're right Minerva, I know you are but I do find it difficult not to worry, I'm afraid.'

Minerva was tempted to reach for more brandy but with the long drive home ahead of them she was feeling sensible enough not to. 'Isis, we're going home today…think about that. Think about Gerald and his loving arms waiting for you, the wonders of the flesh and making up for lost time. Haven't you missed him?'

'Of course I have.' Isis stared at her sandals and wriggled her toes. 'Do you think he feels the same? We haven't spoken at all since I've been here.'

'Well that's hardly surprising is it? We *are* in the back of beyond, the phone signal's rubbish and I haven't spoken to David either if that's any consolation. Anyway, it doesn't do any harm to have some time off from someone now and again. It gives a relationship time to breathe. I think it's a good thing.'

'Do you? I'm never quite sure with Gerald.'

'Why's that? You don't think he's like Derek do you?'

'No of course not! But we haven't been together *that* long and it's all happened so fast. And having this time apart does make me wonder.'

'About what? There you go again, Isis, worrying about nothing! When are you going to just relax and trust in the magic of life? Otherwise you'll just drive yourself mad.'

She was right, thought Isis, but it didn't stop the niggling in her stomach and hadn't Minerva always told her to trust her gut? Her gaze fell upon the red velvet pouch by the kettle.

'Can I pick a card?'

Minerva nodded and handed the cards to Isis who began to shuffle awkwardly, and immediately, a card flew out of the deck.

'I do love a wild card,' said Minerva, 'Adds to the power!'

'Does it?'

Isis looked at the card lying right next to Didge under the table and froze. She looked up at Minerva, 'I can't do it...pick it up I, mean.'

'Oh for Goddess sake, Isis, he won't hurt you.'

Isis was unconvinced and watched Minerva as she ducked under the table and popped up again with the card in her hand. Isis didn't take her eyes off the card or Minerva as she turned it over on the table.

Minerva looked at the three swords piercing through the bright red heart in front of her. 'Well, there's a turn up for the books.'

'It doesn't look good does it?' said Isis, trying to ignore the sinking feeling in her stomach. 'Be honest, Minerva.'

'Oh I always am, Isis, you know that. But as painful as it looks, it's necessary, I'm afraid.'

Isis clasped both hands together and pushed them against her mouth. 'You mean it has to happen?'

'I'm afraid it does by the look of things,' she sighed. 'The Three of Swords is never an easy situation to bear, it's the darkest hour before the dawn in many ways. But things always brighten up afterwards.'

'But they get worse before they get better?'

'Yes, they do.'

She pointed to the rest of the cards Isis was holding.

'This one,' said Isis taking the top card and placing it face upwards on the table.

Minerva drew her breath in sharply as she looked at the card. 'Well, there's a challenge if ever I saw one, Isis. The Seven of Swords is not an easy card by any means…' she paused, 'Basically, it's about not facing up to something, a deception of some kind. And where there's deceit you will always find confusion because that's the nature of it – it's like a dark shadow appearing. And this chap is running away from it do you see?'

Isis peered at the card. 'What exactly is he running away from?'

'One more card, Isis,' prompted Minerva, wondering who *he* could be.

Gingerly, Isis pulled one more and handed it to Minerva, watching her face with great intensity as she turned it over. One eyebrow shot up and with a slow intake of breath, Minerva studied the image in front of her. 'Well, I know it doesn't look good…' she said.

'No it doesn't,' said Isis, 'Struck down by all those swords wouldn't do anyone any good would it? And all that blood makes me feel quite sick.'

'The Ten of Swords is another one of those cards I'm afraid, which may not be a bundle of laughs but has to happen before one can move on.'

'One of those growth cards is it?' Isis shuffled in her seat, 'And growth isn't always comfortable, as you say…'

Minerva looked at her. 'You took the words right out of my mouth, Isis. Glad to hear that some of my magical ramblings do actually stick!'

Isis sat up straight and squared her shoulders. 'I may be a slow learner but it does sink in eventually. But being stabbed in the back isn't nice at all is it?'

'All the more reason to prepare oneself for the event should it occur,' said Minerva. 'Nothing is set in stone and just because you've picked this card, doesn't mean to say it will happen. In fact, it could just as easily have happened already. Derek and his dark exploits could still be hanging around your aura if you ask me.'

'I want to believe that, really I do, but…'

'No buts' about it, Isis. Believe what you like of course, but remember you attract what you focus on and if you're constantly thinking about impending disaster, then don't be surprised if it happens! How we see things is how we experience them if that makes sense. Talking of seeing things…'

She walked over to the kitchen window to see Spit and Polish charging up and down the field, heads and tails in the air.

'What is it?' said Isis straining to look past Minerva.

'Not what but who would be more appropriate, I'd say. The old girl's back.'

Isis gasped. 'Oh, Aunt Crow!'

Minerva swung round. 'Calm down and keep your hair on Isis. Trust in the magic and all will be well. Put the kettle on and make a nice pot of tea, it'll be good for your nerves.'

Isis nodded and sprang into action while Minerva gathered up the tarot cards and carefully put them back in the pouch. She couldn't help noticing the card jutting out at an angle, it was too much of a temptation to miss.

The Death card didn't frighten her. The Grim Reaper was just a messenger and in this case, the right one of course. The only thing missing from the picture was a parrot, which was perfectly understandable. Roger was well and truly on the other side.

They wouldn't be hearing from him again that's for sure.

20

In the Bag

Ronnie looked at Joe as he passed her the flyer. The Planet Reapers stood out in bold black capitals with a picture of the band underneath at one of their recent gigs. It had Allan Key in it, playing the drums and looking like the cat who'd got the cream.

Her eyes scrolled down to the text. 'Six gigs?'

'I know, how about that? He's done us proud has Allan, it's not what you know, eh Ron?'

'They're halfway across the country.'

'Yeah, but all in the same area and only over the course of a week. I won't be away any longer than that. What do you take me for, some kind of nomad?'

He grabbed Morrigan's rag doll propped up on the deck between them, and tickled her with it.

She shot him a serious look. 'Where are you going to stay?'

'Not really sure yet, but Allan's got it all sorted. He knows a lot of pub landlords, so we might end up sleeping on a pub floor somewhere.'

'Living the high life, then? I'm surprised Mr. Key doesn't

have a few hoteliers on his contact list.'

Joe pulled away from her. 'No need to be like that, Ron. I'm just grateful for someone in the band who's got a bit of initiative. Allan may not be Harvey Goldsmith but he knows more people than myself and the rest of the band put together and he's helping us get out there which has to be better than sticking round here playing the same old venues all the time. Surely you can see that can't you?'

Ronnie sighed. 'Yes, I suppose so, if it's what you want to do I can't stop you can I?'

'You wouldn't want to would you? It's not as if I'm swanning off over the other side of the world or anything, it's just a few pub gigs. And anyway, you could come with me if you wanted to.'

She laughed at him. 'Oh and like that's an option! You know I couldn't, not with all the things going on here. I have a child, Joe, and animals to look after!'

He got up and pulled out his tobacco pouch. 'I know that.'

'You can't expect me to drop everything just like that. And you wouldn't want me to come anyway.'

She watched his face as he lit up his smoke and sat down again. 'Look Ron, I'd have no objections if you wanted to come along too. I'm sure you'd enjoy it, but...'

'It's a boys only trip, right?'

'I wouldn't put it quite like that.'

'No of course not. Just no wives or girlfriends, eh?'

Joe shrugged. 'You can think what you like.'

Ronnie picked up the rag doll and began to re-arrange its mop of woollen hair as Joe stared out across the river in silence. Feeling waves of guilt creeping over her she sighed heavily and threw the doll down. 'Look, I'm *sorry*. Ignore me. You do what you want, with who you want. I'm just being stupid.'

'I wouldn't say that, just over-reacting a bit maybe, but you're not stupid. You're anything but that. Look, can we stop all this? I can't make you trust me, but do you think I'd really risk losing what I care about most? You know how much the music means to me, but if you're gonna' get so upset about it, I won't go – simple as that.'

'I don't expect you to do that so please *don't* all right? Not on my account, not on *any* account. I know how much it means to you, of course I do. Go! You've always wanted to get your songs out to more people, and if Allan Key can help do that, good for him.'

'No Ron, it's good for the *band* can't you see that?'

She looked at him and nodded. 'Yeah, I see it, I'm sorry. I'll be fine here, honestly.'

He tilted his head and looked up at her. 'Sure about that?'

'I'm sure.'

'That's all right then.'

As he pulled her close to him, she gave in to the warmth of his skin and the solidness of his body and tried to believe her own words.

* * *

Minerva lifted the last of the bags out of the boot and paid the taxi driver before Aunt Crow did. Somehow it made her feel better about Roger's demise, although she wouldn't dream of doubting the spell they had cast only hours before. A full six hours to mature was more than enough, she thought, as she looked up at the midday sunshine. Now was the time to see it in action. Solar magic was always quick to take effect, particularly as it moved through its daily cycle much faster than the moon did.

Balance was all important and as much as Minerva honoured the Goddess in all her guises, she had great respect for the God. His was a power never to be taken lightly, for without a healthy respect for it one could easily be burned by those rays. It wasn't a pretty sight. She'd seen it happen a few times and it was the very thing which had prompted her to learn how to harness the power of the sun God and use it wisely. Corpse magic was never easy, which was why accurate timing was so important and she prided herself on getting it right. It didn't bear thinking about otherwise.

'There you are, Minerva! You don't know how much we've looked forward to coming home.'

Aunt Crow was still inside the taxi as Minerva unloaded the luggage from the boot. While Isis piled up the bags onto a wheelbarrow, she helped her aunt out of the car and smiled, 'Welcome back, Aunt Crow. Spellstead Hall is not quite the same place without you in it. How was your trip?'

'Very up and down, which is what you'd expect from being on the water,' said Aunt Crow, surveying the land. 'That's Norway off the bucket list anyway, I'm glad we went though. I always did have a hankering for its frilly coastline and a sniff of those Norse Gods which I have to say, are a mighty bunch. But it's good to be back…we've missed the old place, haven't we Roger?'

Aunt Crow turned her head to her right shoulder and Minerva gave Isis a look of triumph before turning back to her aunt. 'I take it Roger enjoyed himself too? He's very quiet.'

'Oh yes,' said Aunt Crow, 'Norway has had the strangest effect on him, would you believe he hasn't said a word for days now?'

Minerva shot a warning look at Isis who stood hanging onto the wobbling wheelbarrow with her mouth open.

'He's looking well enough and so are you, Aunt Crow,' said Minerva. 'How nice to have the chance to really relax and let the world go by, especially the world of the Norse gods, as you say. What better way of experiencing them than in their homeland?'

The three of them made their way down the drive, passing a very exuberant Spit and Polish who continued to charge up and down the paddock fence, heads and tails held high.

'Hello my darlings!' cried Aunt Crow, 'Yes, we've missed you too, haven't we Roger?'

Isis had her eyes fixed firmly on Aunt Crow's right shoulder willing herself to see a parrot. But the more she tried, the less Roger appeared and by the time they reached the house she reluctantly accepted the fact that the dead bird would remain invisible. Aunt Crow was clearly experiencing something completely different but it was obviously how it was supposed to be. They hadn't spent all that time in a ditch at the crack of dawn for nothing. The spell was working and Minerva was right, you didn't question magic, as long as it worked.

Minerva, however, was having to think very quickly on her feet. If Aunt Crow believed Roger was with her and had been all along, he'd better not be sitting in his cage ready to greet her as she walked in otherwise things could get very messy.

She stopped at the front door. 'Aunt Crow, would you mind waiting a moment? There's something I've forgotten to do.'

'Oh Minerva, spare me the pomp and ceremony. I can smell Brenda from here if that's what you mean, and believe it or not I've missed that too. Now out of the way before I open the

door myself. This old stick has many uses, you know!'
She tapped her walking stick against the door and frowned.

Isis appeared suddenly from the rear and barged her way past Aunt Crow and Minerva, flinging the door wide open before disappearing inside and closing it behind her.

'What's she doing?' said Aunt Crow.

'She's reading my mind, that's what she's doing,' said Minerva under her breath. 'It's all right, Aunt, and you're absolutely right about Brenda. The smell is horrendous and poor Isis is quite allergic to the fumes, the only thing that combats them is a good old waft of Faeries in the Forest which has to be lit before the fresh air gets in and circulates around the place.

Aunt Crow narrowed her eyes at Minerva. 'What are you talking about? I've never heard of anything so ridiculous.'

'Believe me, it's true! Isis suffers with her chest, she's not quite as tough as us old boots I'm afraid. Just give her a minute or two and we can go in.'

'Well I never,' said Aunt Crow, leaning on the handle of her stick. 'What do you think of that, eh Roger?

Minerva could've sworn she heard something, but it wasn't a parrot shrieking, it was Isis. She knew what Isis was doing, or at least she thought she did. She willed her to be quiet and do what had to be done quickly as she wouldn't be able to keep Aunt Crow outside for much longer. A crash followed by more shrieks filtered out from inside and Minerva forced a smile at Aunt Crow. It had all been going so well.

Isis had never held anything dead before, in fact it was only in the last few days she'd *seen* anything dead. Removing Roger from the cage was not easy by any means as he was still very much attached to his perch. 'So much for you going to the great perch in the sky,' she whined, 'I can't get you off this one!'

Isis tugged and pulled at the stiff and feathery Roger, but he would not move, and she was beginning to panic.

'Did you find the matches, Isis?' called Minerva from the other side of the door.

'Matches?'

'For the Faeries in the Forest, they're in the kitchen!'

Isis gave one last tug and Roger came free in her hands. 'Oh!' she cried, glancing at the bird as she flew to the kitchen. 'Yes, the incense…'

She could hear her heart pounding through her ears as she scanned the kitchen for the Faeries in the Forest and a hiding place for Roger. The first thing she saw was Minerva's bag and shoving the bird inside, she snatched the green packet of incense and matches from the window sill and ran back into the hall putting all thoughts of brown paper bags to the back of her mind.

Aunt Crow stamped her stick hard against the ground. 'She's taking her time isn't she?'

It was not a good start for a homecoming, and Minerva could have kicked herself for not thinking it through enough. It was obvious now that Roger's stuffed presence wasn't as necessary as she thought it was, especially as he'd made such a good comeback in spirit form. She hoped Isis had made sure he was out of sight, and when the door burst open to reveal a triumphant Isis, she breathed a sigh of relief.

'There!' cried Isis, pointing to the other end of the hallway. 'The Faeries in the Forest are waiting for you in the kitchen, Aunt Crow.'

'I'm glad to hear it, but I'm well and truly used to my Brenda's aromatic tendencies, thank you very much. I'm only sorry you're not, Isis.'

Minerva glared at Isis. 'Those faeries always seem to do the trick don't they? It's always worse about this time of day, don't you think, Isis?'

'You're probably right, yes.'

Aunt Crow was walking hastily towards the kitchen. 'Brenda, take no notice of this pair, it's all a lot of fuss and bother over nothing!'

Minerva turned to a quivering Isis. 'That was a close shave, well done. I thought for one dark and doom filled moment all our work was undone. But you managed to think on your feet, and it looks like it's all in the bag.'

'How did you know?' said Isis.

'What?'

'Roger!'

'Where?'

'In the bag...your bag.'

Minerva glanced across to the table as they entered the kitchen, and back again at Isis. There was no time to say anything, which was just as well, a dead parrot in your handbag wasn't the most inspirational topic at the best of times. They'd have to wait until the journey home, which, as far as Minerva was concerned, couldn't come soon enough.

Holidays were definitely overrated.

21

Into the Cauldron

Aunt Crow bent over her stick, one hand on top of the other. 'I'm so glad you had a nice time here at Spellstead. It's such a weight off the mind when you know there's someone looking after your home and animals who knows what they're doing. I'm very grateful. We both are, aren't we Roger?'

She smiled at her right shoulder and Minerva smiled hesitantly at Aunt Crow. 'No problem at all, Aunt, glad to be of help. And yes of course, anytime you need me again, just shout.'

She threw the last holdall into the back of Mr. Morris, smiling at the blow up mattress in its battered cardboard box hiding at the back, and sighed. A night away in the woods would be the perfect reunion date with David.

'Thank you Minerva,' said Aunt Crow, 'That means a lot to us.'

She smelt of Faeries in the Forest and a faint lingering of flatulence, and Minerva hugged her carefully, avoiding her right shoulder. She sent out a silent prayer of thanks to the

Gods for their assistance in matters of the flesh (or feathers in this case), and for their continued support. However, at the next dark moon she would repeat the spell to keep it going. With the deceased bird in her safe-keeping it would certainly make things easier. Sympathetic magic worked so much better that way.

Patting her bag, she looked around for Isis who was over at the paddock gate with the llamas. Minerva frowned when Isis squealed and jumped back from the two woolly headed monsters while Aunt Crow cackled loudly, 'Such an affectionate pair aren't they? They're just saying goodbye!'

Minerva wrinkled her nose in disgust. 'Well I certainly won't be saying goodbye to them, that's for sure. I've never known such atrocious manners in an animal. Brenda's flatulence is bad enough but Spit is the absolute pits when it comes to bodily fluids! Sorry Aunt, but you know me, I speak as I find. Stinking globules of llama slime is not my idea of a good wash no matter how much Polish thinks otherwise. Besides that, a good time was had by all.'

Aunt Crow smirked. 'I'd get going if I were you, Minerva, before you dig a nice big hole for yourself.'

For an awkward moment, Minerva thought her aunt had seen the ritual ditch, although she *did* remember filling it in afterwards. 'Oh yes, I'm good at that,' she said, and signalling for Isis to wait, she scrambled across to the driver's side before taking her place behind the wheel.

After only three attempts, Mr. Morris submitted to the start-up spell and spluttered off down the drive. A quick glance in the rear mirror showed Aunt Crow cheerily waving with her left hand, her other hand on her right shoulder as if she were holding onto something. She was smiling, and as far as

Minerva was concerned, that was all that mattered. Fixing her eyes on the road ahead, she tightened her grip on the wheel and sighed. 'All I can say is thank the Goddess for small mercies and magic.'

'Yes,' said Isis, 'you were right. It worked.'

'Of course it did,' said Minerva, squinting at the sunshine, 'I knew it would.'

* * *

The journey back was a chilly one. Driving with the windows open was not Minerva's idea of fun but a necessary evil under the circumstances. A passenger stinking of llama slime was the last thing any driver wanted at the beginning of a cold English winter. That wasn't to say that leaving Isis at the first service station hadn't crossed Minerva's mind, but she was too much of a good friend to do it.

However, even with the open windows, the fresh air did nothing to eliminate the stench, in fact it made it worse. And as it circulated around the cozy interior of Mr. Morris, Minerva silently promised him she would give him a thorough clean out when they got home.

'Isis, it's no good, you're going to have to try and wash some of that awful slime off. I can't stand it. Do you have any cleansing wipes on you?' Minerva shouted against the prevailing wind.

'Is it that bad?' screeched Isis, her face contorted by the latest attack of nerves.

'Good Goddess, can't you smell it? It's the foulest stink ever!'

'Worse than Brenda and her…?'

'Yes! Worse than Brenda's arse! Now please, Isis, have a

look for something, *anything* which might help to mask or extinguish it. Otherwise, you're out!'

Isis could see that Minerva wasn't joking and after scrambling about in her bag, proceeded to rub the dried slime from her face and neck with a crumpled tissue. 'Is that any better?' she cried.

'No!' shouted Minerva, 'It needs to be something *wet* to get the stuff off...have a look in my bag.'

Isis didn't like the urgency in Minerva's voice. It only made her anxiety worse, and picking up the purple bag she shoved her hand in and pulled out one deceased parrot. 'ARGH!' she screamed, hurling Roger onto the dashboard.

'That bloody parrot!' cried Minerva. 'As if it hasn't caused enough trouble already. Can you take it OFF the dashboard, Isis. The last thing Mr. Morris needs is a dead parrot on his walnut dash - it's bad enough with this awful bloody smell! I thought we'd left all that chaotic energy behind us. It's no good, we'll have to make a pit stop, I could really do with a strong coffee couldn't you?'

Isis was thinking of something stronger but thought better of it. 'Er yes, I could do with a strong *something*. And where shall I put this?'

She held the dead parrot as far away as she could, shutting her eyes tight.

'Put him back in the bag for now, Isis. I'll find a final resting place for him once I'm back at Crafty Cottage. I've never been so glad to have an animal stuffed, imagine the stench if he wasn't? Dead parrot and llama slime! Poor Mr. Morris, he doesn't deserve to be put through such a vile experience. The worst thing he's ever had to endure is little Morrigan when she's needed her nappy changing or been sick...but this... it's a different kettle of stinking fish altogether, isn't it?'

Isis hung her head. 'I shouldn't of gone to say goodbye to Spit and Polish.'

'There's no point in harping on about that now. What's done is done. Let's stop and refill our tanks with plenty of caffeine and chocolate and hopefully that'll help us get through the rest of the journey, it's not far now. It'll be gone in a breeze, you'll see.'

'There's definitely a strong breeze in here at the moment.'

'Yes, I'm glad the wind spirits have joined us but I wonder if there's anything we can buy from these services to get rid of the smell? They usually have an assortment of stores in these places don't they?'

An hour and two cups of very strong coffee later, as well as a packet of jaffa cakes and two walnut whips, Minerva and Isis were back in Mr. Morris wearing their newly acquired purchases.

'That was a turn up for the books, Isis. Who'd have thought we'd find urban air masks with carbon filters in a service station of all places?

'If you think they'll do the job…' came the muffled reply.

Minerva glanced across at the wide eyes peering over the billowing orange mask and snorted, 'It's got to be worth a try Isis, don't you think?'

'As long as I can still breathe!'

'Of course you can still breathe, it's got holes in. Can you still smell the stench?'

'I can only just about breathe, Minerva!'

'Oh that's all right then, you can't smell anything. I have the faint traces of it wafting underneath this mask but it's not nearly as bad as it was before, thank the Goddess.'

'Wouldn't a packet of pegs be just as useful?' wheezed Isis.

'Don't be daft, that means we'd have to keep our mouths open which means we'd still be exposed to the circulating filth. Do you know how quickly bacteria multiplies, Isis?'

'I thought it was the smell that's offending you!'

'Yes it was, but when you think about it, the whole thing isn't particularly hygienic is it? It comes from the inside of a bloody llama for god's sake!'

'Whatever you say, Minerva,' said Isis, wearily.

'Do you have the other hag stone we picked up?' bellowed Minerva through the mask.

'I think so.'

Isis rummaged in her bag and pulled out the purple drawstring pouch and handed it to Minerva, who took the stone and cupping it in both hands, began to recite the magical words once again:

'Hag of day and hag of night
Imbued with power and sacred light
From above and to the ground, Inside out and turn around
Good for travel, good for health
Be you known and show yourself!'

She placed the stone on the walnut dashboard in front of them and turned to Isis. 'That should do it. Nothing like a good dose of clearance magic when you need it.'

Isis gripped the edge of her seat. 'And how will *that* show itself?'

'Good question. One never knows how these things will play out, but rest assured our journey will now be free of stench and contagion. I wouldn't be surprised if the elements chipped in for good measure. There you are, look at that nice black cloud up there. Water is such a good cleanser.'

Isis looked up and groaned. 'With all this ventilation, that means we're going to get wet!'

'A drop of rain won't hurt you,' snorted Minerva. 'Think of what it's getting rid of. To be cleansed and purified by the water spirits is the perfect remedy for this ugly problem if you ask me!'

Isis slid down further into her seat, shutting her eyes and bracing herself for the inevitable cleansing from the elements while Minerva started up Mr. Morris. They continued the rest of the journey silenced by the wind and water spirits, according to Minerva, while Isis failed to see it in quite the same light. Either way, they were battered by the storm and propelled home in no time.

It was a soggy end to a holiday but not an unwelcome one as far as Minerva was concerned. She may have failed to convince Isis, but the reality of it when they arrived back that evening, was that the stench of llama slime was considerably less than it had been at the start. Soaked to the skin and bordering on hypothermia, they may have been, but stinking they were not.

'Thank heavens for hag stones and hail.'

Minerva leaned against the steering wheel and peeling the soggy mask off, turned to her silent companion. 'We're home, Isis. Are you still in the land of the living or have you slipped between the worlds into an urban mask wasteland? It happens very easily at this time of year.'

There was the slightest movement as Isis fluttered back into life, her mask clinging to her cheeks. 'What time of year is it?' she croaked.

'Samhain, the festival of the dead, remember?'

Isis didn't answer at first, putting all her energy into wiggling her fingers. 'I think I've been on the edge of that world you're talking about. *I'm so cold!*'

'Right, let's get in and get dried off and warmed up,' barked Minerva, jumping out and throwing her damp mask on the drive. 'Come on Isis, before you end up over the other side completely. You're not looking your best, I have to say, although nothing that a nice hot toddy won't put right.'

She dragged the trembling and soaking passenger out of Mr. Morris and into Crafty Cottage accompanied by much grunting and groaning. However, before long they were sat in front of a hastily made fire, sipping from steaming mugs of brandy laced with lemon and honey. They stared at Roger, propped awkwardly on the mantelpiece to dry out, his feathers stuck in wet clumps to his scrawny body beside a flickering tealight.

'Will it affect his stuffing?' said Isis, sounding almost human again.

'You mean the wet? I hope not,' said Minerva. 'Let's hope Mr. Stuffham did a good enough job and it's only his feathers the rain has ruffled.'

Isis nodded and sipped at the warm brandy. '*We're* the ones who've had the stuffing knocked out of us.'

Minerva shot her a sidelong glance. 'Speak for yourself. I'm warming up very nicely, thank you. Get it down you, Isis, we'll sleep well tonight!'

'What about David? Aren't you going to tell him you're back?'

'I'll ring him in the morning. I could do with the time to get my bearings, and besides, I've just remembered his mother is over from Ireland. He'll be fussing over her at the moment.'

'Or she'll be fussing over *him*.'

Minerva thought about that for a moment, 'You've got a point there, Isis. I'm not really looking forward to meeting her at all, if I'm honest. A Witch and a staunch catholic are not the most harmonious of combinations are they?'

* * *

Warmed by the brandy and the crackling fire in the hearth, the two friends drifted into silence. The only other sound was the slow ticking of the Green Man clock above the mantelpiece accompanied by a gently snoring Isis. Minerva smiled as she looked at her friend. It wasn't surprising she should drift off first, all those frayed nerve endings must leave one frazzled, literally. Thank the Goddess she didn't have the same problem. However, she was glad to be home and as thoughts of David seeped through the hazy numbness, the phone rang, stirring her out of it.

'David…' she breathed softly into the mouthpiece, 'How lovely.'

'How was your trip?'

'It was eventful,' she said, glancing at the mantelpiece and the snoozing Isis. 'But, yes, Aunt Crow enjoyed her holiday, and we got back in one piece, so all's well that ends well, I suppose. Where are you, the vicarage?'

'Where else would I be?'

She rubbed her eyes. 'It's wonderful to hear your voice.'

'Ditto,' he paused, 'My mother's here…'

'And Isis is here,' she glanced at the Green Man's ticking face. 'It's almost midnight.'

He laughed softly, 'Ah yes, the Witching hour, I just wanted to check you got back safely. We'll see each other tomorrow.'

'That's in a few minutes,' she could feel her pulse racing. 'David, we won't have any time tomorrow…not on our own. Why don't we meet *now* in the graveyard?'

'You're a terrible tease, Minerva.'

'What do you expect, ringing me at this hour after all this time apart? I'll see you in five minutes.'

She snuffed out his laughter in one push of a button and sprang out of her chair. Grabbing her coat and checking in the hallway mirror, she left a snoring Isis and made her way round to the vicarage, popping an extra strong mint into her mouth as she went.

* * *

He was standing by the biggest Yew tree in the graveyard. An owl hooted among the tall Poplars standing like watch towers, and she smiled at the faint silver crescent of a new moon in the sky. She'd always felt at home in graveyards, often wandering in and out of the stones, mesmerized by the names and dates, and wondering about the lives of those who lay beneath them.

'It feels very magical to be here…' she sighed, sinking into his arms, 'with you, and the ancestors.'

'We're certainly in the minority, that's for sure,' he whispered, tugging her hair free from the velvet scrunchie and kissing her neck.

'But if we died here with them right now, together, it would be a total spiritual experience wouldn't it?'

'I'm not so sure about that. Ivy Bitchamen's right beside us and she was far from spiritual, god bless her.'

Minerva turned and looked down at the shiny black marble

stone and the clump of decaying chrysanthemums lying in front of it. 'Oh yes, I remember her. She was the one who set light to the scarecrow wedding party in the churchyard the other year wasn't she?'

'That's right. My first trimester in the parish and an arsonist to deal with of all things.'

'Didn't she..?'

'Unfortunately, she did. I'm not sure if she meant to go that way but that's the way it went, sadly. Didn't stand a chance. She was an unsteady old dear anyway and must have spilled a fair amount of the paraffin over herself before taking a match to the lot.'

Minerva winced. 'Oh my Goddess, sounds like she was unsteady in more ways than one.'

David nodded. 'Her husband left her, I believe, which didn't help her *or* the wedding party as it turned out.'

Minerva turned to him. 'I remember now...fifty years together down the drain after a night out with Moonlight Sally from Allsorts and Escorts. It sent Ivy quite doolally. And why wouldn't she pick on the wedding party? It stands to reason after all, doesn't it? Her sacred vows and all those years reduced to a cheap night out on the town.'

'It didn't turn out cheap for Ivy, she paid with her life.'

They stood wrapped in each others arms and said nothing. It was difficult to imagine a fate worse than Ivy's at that moment, although there were plenty more endings to ponder over right under their noses.

David pulled Minerva close. 'Are you all right?'

She nodded. 'Is the shed open?'

He smiled at the small building beyond the gravestones and pulled out a set of keys. 'As luck would have it, yes. What did you have in mind, a roll in the wheelbarrows?'

She winked at him. 'We could park them outside.'

David took her hand and walked towards the shed hidden in the shadows by the overhanging Yews. The sound of a slowly dripping tap as it filled an old watering can was quite hypnotic in the dark. The metal bin full of dead flowers next to it didn't quite have the same appeal but it didn't matter one bit.

Minerva smiled. 'It doesn't get much more romantic than this does it, vicar? Here we are outside under the stars with garden sheds and…' she glanced at the compost bin, 'dead flowers. It's all very Lady Chatterley!'

David chuckled as the door creaked open. 'I suppose I could easily slip into the boots of…what was his name?'

'Mellors! Yes I think you could, but first, you need to slip out of this.'

She pulled at his dog collar, searching for the fastener.

Wheelbarrows were pushed aside, clamped tight to the shed wall alongside spades and forks, as David slung his jacket down. They tumbled onto the damp floor, tearing at each other's clothes in their urgency to swap the mundane world for the magical. In the realms of fleshy delights Minerva embraced her inner Lady Chatterley, fuelled by the forbidden fruits of fantasy. And David too, indulged in their reunion, casting aside his spiritual vocation for the physical, earthier one of Mellors.

Not surprisingly, it didn't last long. Need is like that. It doesn't wait around for permission, but drives itself mad until it gets what it wants. And when it's done, it fades and forgets, until the next time.

'Did you miss me?' said Minerva, watching a beetle scurrying across the floor.

'Couldn't you tell?

She groaned softly. 'I don't want this night to end. Imagine if we stayed here until the morning, and watched the sun rise over the gravestones. Wouldn't it be magical?'

'I'm not sure Alfie Waller from the village would think so when he opens up for the first dig of the day. I've got two funerals tomorrow and both are burials.'

'Hmm,' she mused, 'maybe not the best of wake up calls for either party, eh vicar? It was a nice thought anyway. Seven of Cups to be precise, according to the tarot.'

'Which is?' said David, brushing the cobwebs out of her hair.

'The difference between fantasy and reality, all those castles in the air,' she said dreamily. 'What would you choose?'

Without replying, he jumped up and went outside, returning with one hand behind his back and a hint of a boyish grin. Bowing deeply at her feet, he presented a very tired looking rose, still in its pot. 'You, my dear Goddess…I would choose you. Pardon the almost dead flower but it's the only one out there still alive.'

Minerva was stunned. What was he saying? And did it involve a ring or a handfasting? Or both? She felt for the label around the scrawny stem and twisted it to get a closer look at the name.

'Well?' he said, watching her expression change from shock to amusement in the dim light of the church torch. 'Pray tell me the name of this almost dead flower destined for the compost heap. I have a feeling there is great power in it, as you always say.'

'If ever there was a plant so aptly named for me right now,' she teased, 'it would be this.'

David pulled the rose towards him, peering at the label. And there, stamped in fading black capitals was the name: *CHAOS MAGIC*. Minerva watched as the look of disbelief turned to laughter and they fell, like the dead flowers, into a heap beside it.

'So pray tell me, vicar, what do you choose me for?' she asked, her heart pounding.

He hesitated, 'Ah, that's for me to know and for you to find out, my Goddess of Chaos!'

'Oh David, that's not fair!'

'What's the rush anyway? Looks like our God and Goddess have already made their minds up for us,' he nodded at the rose. 'Can't we savour the magic a little longer?'

He was right of course, she knew that. Rings and ceremonies were only the icing on the cake, after all.

'I bow to your innate wisdom,' she told him in hushed tones, 'But I'll tell you this, whatever you choose…one lifetime will never be enough.'

He grinned. 'Only a witch would say such a thing.'

'And only a vicar,' she whispered, 'could change her mind.'

She wondered if it really mattered.

Wasn't love the most powerful spell of all? Time would tell, perhaps, but for now the words were out, the die was cast and by the magic they were bound.

Afterword

I hope you enjoyed the story as much as I loved writing it. If you have a couple of minutes to leave an honest review on Amazon – just a few words would be great –
I'd really appreciate it.
For news, updates on future books and a free copy of Black Dogs and Broomsticks (prequel to the Madness and Magic series)
sign up for the Treehouse Magic Newsletter.
www.sheenacundy.com

About the Author

Songwriter. Storyteller. Sheena Cundy is a teacher of horse and rider, reader of the Tarot and a Reiki Master.

Since childhood, my love of horses and the healing and magical arts has never waned and continues to filter into my writing any which way it can.

The Madness and the Magic is the debut novel I wrote to keep out of prison, a straitjacket and the divorce courts while battling with murderous tendencies and all kinds of hormonal horrors during a mid-life crisis. Bonkers and Broomsticks is the sequel and Chaos in the Cauldron is number three in the series...

Apart from Witch Lit and other magical fiction, I also write spiritual non-fiction and sing and write the songs for my pagan band, **Morrigans Path.**

You can connect with me on:
- https://sheenacundy.com
- https://twitter.com/OrgSheena
- https://www.facebook.com/SheenaCundyAuthor
- https://www.instagram.com/treehouse_witch

Subscribe to my newsletter:
- https://www.subscribepage.com/blackdogs

Printed in Great Britain
by Amazon